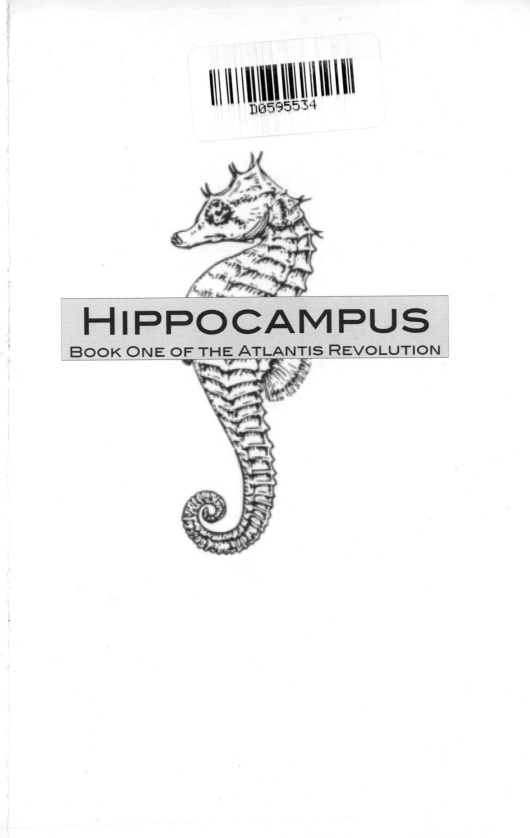

HIPPOCAMPUS
BOOK ONE OF THE ATLANTIS REVOLUTION

"…an original, well-crafted story!"
-Kevin Wong on Inkpop

2010 Textnovel.com Editor's Choice

"…Great characters, written into a highly imaginative storyline."
-Famlavan on Authonomy

"Watch out Harry Potter, here comes Trey Atlas. An imaginative beginning of what could become the next YA epic series."
-Kidd 1 on Authonomy

2010 Textnovel.com Contest Semi-Finalist

"Brilliant."
-Star Gazer on Inkpop

"I love the world you've created. Your writing is descriptive, clear, and to the point. Excellent imagination."
-Natalie Jones on Authonomy

Top 150 Book on Inkpop in 2010

"…Fantastic."
-A Knight on Authonomy

"Your premise is so incredibly unique. This is a really clever and original book. A great read."
-Carrie L McRae on Inkpop

Myles,

Thank you for joining the Revolution!

HIPPOCAMPUS

BOOK ONE OF THE ATLANTIS REVOLUTION

TOM TANCIN

12/2014

Merry christmas!

Second Edition, January 2014

Summary: The Knights of the Abyss wage war on Atlantis. Sixteen-year-old Trey Atlas is the only one that can stop them from destroying all that Atlantis stands for and, as a result, erasing his own mysterious past.

1. Young Adult—Fiction

2. Fantasy—Fiction

3. Atlantis—Fiction

For more information visit:
www.tomtancin.com
www.theatlantisrevolution.com

For You
Thank you for sharing in this story.

Atlantis exists. Of course, you don't know this because it's hidden from our world. Eleven thousand years ago, the Greeks and Egyptians attacked Atlantis. In order to protect the island, Aruc, a sorcerer, created an illusion of the island sinking and then put a barrier in place to prevent outsiders from seeing or gaining access to Atlantis. But Aruc knew that the isolated island was not safe forever. In fact, he cast the very prophecy that predicted the bleak future of the island. His prophecy became known as Profiteia ek Epanastasi.

From Blood of Evil and Blood of True

A Boy is Born and this Prophecy Due

For When the Abyss Rises to Make Its Mark

The Savior is the Boy with Royal Blood Half Dark

The sorcerer then designed a plan that would ensure the survival of the island he loved. For thousands of years, Atlantis continued in peace and prosperity with no need for the plan.

Sixteen years ago, the Prince foreseen in Aruc's prophecy was born. Familiar with the Prophecy, and knowing that one day the boy would be needed to save Atlantis, the royal family sent the baby off the island to ensure his safety in the world outside Atlantis. Eleven thousand years after it was created, Aruc's plan was finally put in motion.

The Atlantis Revolution begins…

HIPPOCAMPUS
BOOK ONE OF THE ATLANTIS REVOLUTION

Mnemosunero

Royal Palace – Atlantis

Aerian woke with a gasping breath. Her face, drained of all color, contrasted her sweat matted black hair and gray robes. If her dream was true, something that had been predicted eleven thousand years ago was in progress. She listened to the world around her to figure out if she should believe the dream that woke her. But, being deep in the heart of the palace basement, she didn't hear anything at all.

Dark and dungeon-like, the room was special to her none-the-less. Trinkets and other artifacts, reminiscent of her ancestors, cluttered the room. Her family had served the Atlantean royals since the first record of Atlantean time and it just so happened that some of the artifacts in the very room she now occupied were sixty-thousand years old.

One particular artifact was of interest at that moment. The most important one passed down through the family of sorcerers. The one that could clarify the situation. But she wouldn't find it in her room so she climbed out of bed and walked to the door.

A sharp knife tore through her mind like it was flesh and she screamed in agony.

Aerian. The word came to her like a whisper avoiding her ears and going directly to her brain. A feeling of urgency swept through her, probably transferring from the person trying to get her attention. She needed to find them and figure out what was going on.

She closed her eyes and searched her thoughts, as she had been trained to do. A few seconds later, she made the connection and found herself lying on the floor under a bed, looking out at smoke. She saw boots; dark, navy blue boots. The silver symbol on the boots verified that the dream was true.

Aerian forced herself out of the body and looked at the scared face of the blond boy. Dirt covered his smooth features, caked to his face by tears. The bloodshot ocean blue eyes belonged to Prince Maciek, the nine-year-old grandson of the ruling Prince and Princess.

Aerian.

I'm coming, just stay there. She quickly slipped her boots on under her robes and ran out of the dungeon toward the steps that would lead her up to the palace. Her ancestors had predicted this day would come but none of the royals had listened. Now, at seventeen and with powers not fully developed, she had to save the royal family.

She climbed the steps cautiously. Voices from above caused her to stop. Closing her eyes, she concentrated on the hallway at the top of the stairs. Three of them were in the hallway, dressed in navy blue outfits, only their eyes left exposed. The silver symbol of a wave on their headpiece represented the Knights of the Abyss, an underground organization determined to take control of Atlantis.

Founded by individuals with a hatred for the Atlantean kings of the past, the Knights had made it their goal to overthrow a royal family and change the entire structure of the Atlantean government. They had waited for hundreds of years and strategically gained access to the palace and the royal families. The Knights that now threatened the lives of the royal family may have been their guards earlier that afternoon. All of this knowledge had been passed down through the Mnemosunero but, while the sorcerers took it seriously, the royals ignored it.

The searing pain tore through her mind again. She muffled a scream with her hand. The Knights moved closer, their shadows on the steps in front of her. Thankfully, the curved wall kept her hidden from their view.

Using her mind, she took control of the flame of a candle on the stone wall. Pulling her arms apart, she forced the flame into a large wave of fire and bolted up the steps, throwing the fire at the Knights. Orange engulfed navy; the Knights screamed in horror. Waving her hands over the air, she hid their screams until all three succumbed to the flames. The smell of burnt cloth and flesh all that remained.

She breathed heavy, her heart raced, and her head pounded. Mentally and physically exhausted after battling only three Knights, she forced herself to continue.

Her heart dropped. Maciek's mental waves could not be located. Sadness tore through her as she tried to connect with Maciek's older brother, Prince Sandro, but came up empty. The thoughts of their father, Evander, and their mother, Kyra, could not be located either.

A crash downstairs interrupted her before she could focus on the last person with whom she wanted to connect. She headed down toward the crash, which sounded like it came from her room. As she approached the door to the room, she heard movement from inside. Two Knights searched through the artifacts on the shelves.

"Looking for something?" Aerian asked as she stepped into the doorway.

The Knights turned to her and each pulled the sword from the scabbard on their belt. "You don't have to be a sorceress to realize that," one said in a deep, raspy voice.

"But lucky for me," she replied, "I am a sorceress. That would be most unfortunate for you though."

"We're interested in a particular member of the royal family," the Knight with the raspy voice told her. "The one with dark blood. With him in place as King, we'll control the island."

"You'll run our civilization into poverty and depression," Aerian said.

"No worse than these rich, selfish royals have done for the last eleven thousand years," the Knight hissed.

"Where's the boy?" the other Knight grew impatient with her.

"I'm not telling you," Aerian answered.

The Knight with the raspy voice ran forward, grabbed and turned her, and, with his back now to the door, placed the sword to her throat. "You will tell us where he is."

"If you kill me, you'll never find him."

"We'll take that chance," the Knight standing in front of her said. He nodded his head, giving the one with the raspy voice the permission to kill her.

Before he could slice her neck, he let out a gasping moan and fell to the floor. Aerian blasted a wave of energy at the one in front of her, forcing him into the wall. A young man ran toward the Knight that lay on the floor against the wall. He stabbed his sword into the Knight's chest, pulled it out, and turned to face her.

"Jedrick," she hugged him. "I thought you were dead. I was going to connect with you but was interrupted."

His handsome face stained with dirt and blood and his disheveled blond hair showed he had been in a fight. The ocean blue tunic left his upper arms uncovered, revealing a seahorse tattoo on his left arm. His ocean blue eyes stared into her and they kissed.

"I came for you as soon as I could," Jedrick told her. His eyes and voice saddened. "The rest of the family is dead. I searched just about every room. They killed my mom, dad and grandparents."

"Maciek and Sandro?" asked Aerian.

His eyes watered. "My cousins are dead."

"No," she cried. Her stomach twisted and her lungs burned.

"So are all of the servants, who were in the princesses' room."

"And the princesses?"

"All of them are dead," Jedrick told her.

Not knowing herself, she looked to him for guidance. "What do we do now?"

"We get out of the palace and run as far as we can," he said.

"I have to get the...."

"We don't have time. There will be more Knights down here in a matter of minutes. They already eliminated everyone upstairs so they're going to comb the tunnels under the palace to make sure no one escaped. We're next if we don't run now."

He grabbed her arm and pulled her out of the room. They ran as fast as they could.

"Where are we going?"

"The southeastern forest," he said.

Aerian stopped and Jedrick was pulled back as well. "That's too far away. And who knows if the Knights already infiltrated the base."

"Where else are we going to go? Now come on!" He pulled her again but she wouldn't move.

"Jedrick, you're the new ruling Prince. You have to be near so you can run the city."

"They're going to kill me if they find me," he reminded her. "The farther we get from this place, the better. Come on..."

Before they took five steps, Jedrick fell to the ground and screamed in pain. He searched for the object in the back of his ankle and pulled out a throwing star. One of its points dripped with blood from his ankle.

Five Knights approached them, swords in hand. "I'll take my star back," said one of the Knights, reaching for it. Aerian swooped her hands forward and shot a gust of energy at them. It caused them to stumble backwards but didn't knock them over.

"My body is weak," she told Jedrick.

Jedrick made it to his feet, putting all of the pressure on his left, healthy ankle. He pulled the sword from the scabbard on his belt.

"That's the boy," said the Knight who asked for the star.

"Are you sure?" another asked.

"What do you want?" Jedrick questioned.

"All we're asking is that you come with us," the first Knight told him. "We have a proposition for you."

"We'll never go with you," Aerian replied.

"Don't make this difficult," the Knight said. "Our leader needs to speak with the Prince. We have no reason to kill you."

"You think we believe that?" Jedrick said, grating his teeth. "As long as I'm alive, I'm ruler of Atlantis. You want control of the island so you have to kill me."

"We're not trying to take your throne," the Knight told him. "We're just trying to use it."

"Liar! You killed my entire family." Jedrick attacked, the Knight caught Jedrick's sword with his own and the clanging metal echoed down the stone hall.

"Don't kill him," another Knight shouted.

"Are you sure he's the right..." A bullet of energy hit the Knight square in the forehead and he collapsed to the floor with a thud. Aerian's body relaxed after the spell as the other three Knights turned their attention to her and charged. She ran, their footsteps echoing off the walls behind her.

One of the Knights caught up to her and pushed her to the

ground. She used a wave of energy to push him away and scrambled to her feet. A sword sliced her arm, she screamed with the tearing of flesh, and backed against the wall holding the bleeding wound.

"Now tell your boyfriend to come with us," said the Knight holding the sword dripping with her blood.

"No!"

Jedrick hobbled towards them. The Knight he fought now lay on the floor. He stabbed one Knight before he could defend himself and the other two turned to the Prince. They both swiped their swords at Jedrick but he avoided them.

"It's not him," one of the Knights said as he blocked Jedrick's sword.

Aerian ran over and grabbed the sword from the Knight laying on the stone floor. She stabbed one of the two Knights that battled Jedrick and then turned to the last Knight.

Jedrick's face went blank and he let out a gasp of air. The remaining Knight turned his eyes to hers as he pulled the bloody sword from Jedrick's chest. "It wasn't him," the Knight hissed evilly as he bore his eyes into Aerian.

Pain, sorrow, and fear flowed through her as the Knight moved toward her. Clenching her teeth, she gathered up as much strength as she could and shot a bullet of energy at him. The barely visible bullet connected with the Knights' head and he fell.

Aerian dropped to her knees next to Jedrick. She smiled slightly when he gasped for air, though she knew he wouldn't make it much longer without help. She tore the blue tunic, removing the cloth from his chest. The amount of blood that came from the wound turned her stomach ill.

She tried to muster up the power to heal him. "Come on!" she cried. He was dying and she didn't even have the power to save him. "I'm sorry!" The last amount of energy had been used to take down the last Knight. "I'm sorry!" Tears poured from her eyes like teeming rain.

"It's alright," Jedrick comforted her through gasps of air and moans of pain. "You...have the chance...to save..." He struggled to take in enough air to talk. "...Use the plan." He gasped a few more heavy breaths and his eyes turned lifeless.

"No!" Aerian laid her head on Jedrick's stomach. The right side of her face soaked in the blood that had poured out of him. She heard his last statement in her head. *Use the plan.* The perfect idea. If she didn't do it, Jedrick and the rest of the royal family would have died in vain. She sat up. *Use the plan.* She kissed Jedrick

one last time and then pushed herself to her feet. Her stomach

sick; she felt like she could vomit.

She forced her aching, dirty body to walk down the hallway, only able to move slowly at first, but picking up speed as she went. She had to make it to the river that ran under the palace. It was the best way for her to make it to the destination needed to put the plan in play.

By the time she approached the river, she jogged at a nice pace. She jumped in the river and let the currents carry her, saving her strength for what was going to have to take place. It took less than a minute to make it to the royal grounds just outside the palace. She caught the bank of the river and pulled herself out.

The palace walls, like massive sand dunes, hid the murdered bodies of the people she knew and loved. Though not family, they were the closest thing to it she'd ever known. Jedrick's parents had loved her as their own and she loved Jedrick more than she thought she could ever love anyone.

Her legs bent under her, her face nearly touched the ground, as tears, mixed with the little of Jedrick's blood that remained on her face, dropped to the soil. Not a single royal survived the vicious attack. Jedrick had made it clear that he was the last one alive but now he too was dead. More tears ran from her eyes. If only she hadn't used all her power, she could have saved him.

Use the plan.

She couldn't sit and dwell on the tragedy at this point. She had to put the plan in play. She climbed to her feet and walked cautiously toward the temple. The plan had to be activated at the pond right outside the large marble building. Smoke rose out of its roof as she searched the area for Knights. There were none in sight.

Aerian knelt in front of the pond and placed her hand in the water. A sensation of losing all memory took over. She stared in the water, which now glowed with a white light. The water reflected the image of the Knight pulling the sword from Jedrick's chest. The image of Jedrick's death faded to her lighting the Knights on fire. Maciek, under his bed, called for her help. The image faded again. She was a young child, stealing food to eat and sleeping on the streets. She met the young, handsome Jedrick for the first time and he took her to meet his family. The smiles and embraces of acceptance.

Her mind came back to life, giving her more control over what she saw in the water. She discovered the room with the ancient artifacts that she now occupied. That's when she figured out she was a sorceress and a descendant of a long line of sorcerers.

She smiled as Jedrick kissed her for the first time. He had been

so nervous and she had found herself equally nervous after the fact. She hadn't seen it coming and she didn't know how to respond. Three years later, kissing him like that was so easy but it also meant so much more.

Now having complete control over the visions in the water, she searched for an ancient memory. One she did not have herself. A fragment of mind given to the Mnemosunero by her ancestor, Aruc. The memory appeared in the water. Aruc cast a silver jewel, diamond shaped with wings on the side and a blue gem on the top triangle, into the unknown.

Focused on the jewel, she forced her mind to stay with it. She continued moving the memories faster through time until she reached the present. The jewel rested in a box that sat in a dark space. Focusing harder, she hoped the water would show her the person who would next receive the jewel.

The new prince of Atlantis.

Lucky Charm

Miami, Florida

I sat in biology at just past noon. I hoped to make it through the day as quickly as possible so that I could get to swim practice. The teacher, a tall, thin, balding man, paced the room rambling about the projection of the human brain on the screen in front of us.

"Work with your lab partner and use the laptops to find the name of the structure highlighted in red," Mr. Walker instructed. "Also find the meaning of the name and the function of the structure. I want it all on a piece of paper before the bell rings. Get to work."

"Hey Trey," Coal, my lab partner and one of my two best friends, sat down next to me.

Jessica met my eyes with hers and smiled, her white teeth accented by parted pink lips. I couldn't ignore her perfectly groomed red hair or her green eyes that filled with admiration as they stared at me. I smiled back. She looked like she'd just won the lottery as she turned her focus back to the computer in front of her.

Coal waved his hand in front of my face. "Can you go two minutes without attracting the opposite sex?" My smooth, model-worthy face, ocean blue eyes, and layered blond hair made me one of the most popular guys in the school and Coal liked to tease me about it.

"Are you ever going to get past the jealousy, Connor?"

"You know I hate that name." At his request, everyone called him by his nickname. Then again, it did fit him due to his black hair, rough face, and dark eyes.

"When you give me a hard time, I'll call you by your real name. This really isn't anything new." I powered on the Macbook.

"I'm not jealous you know," he said.

"I know, I know. We go through this all the time." Truthfully, while most girls avoided Coal like the plague, he had a steady girlfriend of a few years so he had no reason to be jealous. "Let's just get to work."

"You search Wikipedia and I'll search Answers.com," Coal told me.

"Those aren't reputable sources." I didn't want to lose points for using sources our teacher didn't want us to use. I took pride in my grades and maintained straight "A's".

"So what?" he said. "Let's just get information and be done with it."

I looked back at the image and stared at the pea pod shaped structure highlighted in red. I connected its location to the information

I studied the night before. "It's in the temporal lobe," I informed Coal of my connection. "Looks like it's in the central part of that lobe. That might help us narrow it down."

"Found the temporal lobe on Wikipedia," Coal said. "It's involved in hearing, speech, and vision. It says it includes the hippocampus."

I typed 'hippocampus' into a medical website's search engine. I read the text that appeared once the screen loaded. "The hippocampus is involved in long-term memories."

"And spatial navigation," Coal added.

I clicked the picture on the page and, when it came up enlarged, I studied the portion labeled 'hippocampus'. Sure enough, it looked just like the highlighted structure on the screen.

"That's it," I told Coal. "Write it down."

We recorded that the structure was the 'hippocampus' and that it was involved in long-term memories and spatial navigation.

"Find out what the name means," Coal said.

I searched the term in Answers.com. It broke the term down to Greek roots. "'Hippos' means 'horse' and 'kampos' means 'sea monster'," I read to Coal. "But hippocampus is also the genus name for the seahorse. They call the structure the hippocampus because it reminded the scientists who first studied it of a seahorse."

"I don't think it looks anything like a seahorse," Coal shot me a weird look.

"Did I say I thought that?" I replied. "I said *they* thought that."

We finished recording our findings on our papers and prepared to turn them in. "What're you doing later?" Coal asked.

"I have swim practice, like normal."

"Again?" he replied, sounding annoyed.

"You know the meet is tomorrow and I..."

"Not that," he cut me off. "Jessica's staring you down again. It's amazing she's not drooling."

I turned my attention to her and met her eyes with my best smile. She glowed with exhilaration.

"Seriously dude, cut it out," Coal reprimanded me. "I'm tired of watching them fall at your feet."

"Why are you jealous?" I asked. "You have Sara and she's great."

"Yeah but man, you have every female on the planet at your disposal. You walk by and they practically grovel at your feet for attention. I wish I had that for just a day."

"It's awesome," I assured him, still smiling at Jessica.

"Just last week you went out with Brittany and now you're moving on."

"I'm too busy for the serious relationship stuff," I told him. "I'm good for the casual fling."

"Leave your papers on the counter on your way out," Mr. Walker instructed. "Make sure you read the next section in the book."

The bell rang and I stood up. I pulled my designer jeans up and fixed my shirt. I noticed Jessica, as well as a few other girls, watching every move I made.

"Just ask her out already," Coal complained.

"I can't," I said. "I have the meet tomorrow. I'm so strapped for time. Maybe next week."

"The sad part is, she'll actually wait patiently for you to ask her. Of course she'll stare and drool while she waits." He laughed.

I laughed with him. "Yeah, it sucks being me." We headed for lunch with Jessica walking stalkerishly behind us.

The rest of my day was normal. I said 'bye' to Coal quickly before heading to the pool to meet Coach.

"Trey, you have the chance to go to regionals," Coach gave me the usual pep talk. "Tomorrow you're going to compete in the last swim meet needed to get there. If you win this, you can go to regionals and hopefully, eventually, nationals too."

"I'm ready, Coach," I assured her.

"I know you are. You're the best swimmer I ever coached." I could read it in her green eyes; Coach counted on me. She had been set on getting me to nationals since eighth grade. After all, she didn't have a life outside of our school, which is probably what made her the best math teacher and coach I ever had.

There was more to winning nationals than just fulfilling Coach's dream. As a sophomore, I really wanted to be dubbed the best swimmer in the nation. Plus, our entire school counted on me because we needed to get some positive publicity. We weren't doing well on the mandated state tests and no one from our school stood out academically

Coach told me to go practice and then headed to her office. I went into the locker room and changed into the blue and white swimsuit that represented our team. I put the matching cap on and then walked back to the pool. I put my goggles on and then dove in.

The water was cold but my body quickly acclimated to it. I swam the length of the pool, turned around, and kicked off the wall, heading back to where I started. Seventy-five laps of peace before me, I didn't have to think about anything more than swimming.

Lap number fifty interrupted my concentration. A shadow glided over the pool floor below me. I didn't pay much attention to it

because I concentrated on getting to the other wall. As I approached the wall, bubbles came up and hit me in my stomach. I stopped and looked around. No one was in or around the pool. I dove under and looked at the bottom. Nothing.

I needed to finish the last twenty-five laps so I started swimming again. A blood-curdling scream pierced the water on my second lap. A woman. A scream for help. Coach? I stopped swimming and searched the pool. The scream dissipated and it was quiet again.

Coach sat peacefully at the desk in her office. If it wasn't her, who was it? It did sound like it came from the bottom of the pool. But who can scream like that under water? And there was no one in the pool with me. I had to be imagining things. The water was getting to my brain.

Just to be sure, I dove down to the bottom of the pool and ran my hand on the floor. I didn't see the shadow; I didn't hear the scream. I swam for the surface, took a deep breath, and tried to convince myself that I imagined the whole thing. But I wasn't able to shake it.

I decided I had enough of the pool, which was the first time I ever felt that way. After rinsing the chlorine off and changing into my gym shorts and a t-shirt, I headed to to the gym.

The gym was three blocks from the school. My parents had given me a new Mustang for my sixteenth birthday a few weeks before but I only had a permit and couldn't drive on my own. Besides, walking was great exercise.

The scream kept echoing in my head. Someone, a woman, was being tortured and I didn't know who it was. I tried to convince myself that I couldn't do anything to help. When that didn't work, I tried thinking that it was all just a figment of my imagination.

My regular work out routine and ambition to stay in shape helped me ignore the screams replaying in my head. I had the typical swimmer's body. My arms and legs were toned but they weren't huge. I didn't want to be a body builder, just a healthy athlete.

Push-ups, sit-ups, crunches, weight lifting, squats, and three miles on the treadmill completed my nearly two hours workout but I wasn't done yet. I still had to get home so I gathered my belongings and then, like every other day, ran the mile and half home.

When I got home, the house smelled like a delicious chicken dinner. And indeed, when I went to the kitchen for a bottle of water, I saw that Maria, our housekeeper, was making lemon grilled chicken on the indoor grill appliance sold by that former boxer. I can't remember his name. I think his slogan was "I pity the fool" or something like that.

She was also steaming a California vegetable mix, my favorite, and had a Caesar salad already sitting on the table. "Dinner will be ready in fifteen minutes," she told me with a smile. "Your mother and father will be home in ten."

We had plenty of housekeepers in my life and Maria was the best one we ever had. She was great at keeping the house clean and managing daily duties, her cooking always delicious, and she knew how to operate around a busy, rich family.

"I need to get a shower," I told her. "I'll hurry to be ready by dinner." She nodded and went back to finishing the dinner. I headed upstairs to my room.

My room was larger than any of my friends rooms, at least the ones I'd been in. I had my own private bathroom. My favorite part of my room was the high definition projector and surround sound that allowed me to experience theater quality movies in my own bedroom.

The warm water ran the sweat and griminess off me. I washed off and then shampooed my hair. Water ran in my ear and the scream pierced my brain. I dug at my ear, trying to get the water out. My eardrum felt like it would burst from the woman's high-pitched voice.

Quickly washing the shampoo out of my hair, and turning the shower off, I stepped out, toweled myself off, and then wrapped the towel around my waist. Using a cotton swab, I got the water out of my ear. Once I did, the screaming stopped.

I stood at the mirror, staring into my ocean eyes. The thought hit me like a freight train. The scream was in the water. I heard it when I was in the pool and then when water got in my ear. And, in both cases, the scream seemed to be coming from the water itself.

Maria called me on the intercom to tell me that dinner was on the table and hot. I quickly got changed into my favorite jeans. So what if I paid nearly two hundred dollars for jeans that looked like they went through a war? That was my style. An orange t-shirt that had the slogan, "Miami Made" caught my attention from the hangar. I slipped the shirt on and then put on socks and my

boots.

I went down and found my parents just sitting down to eat. Joining them, I filled my plate as quickly as possible. I was starving and it smelled great.

"Are you ready for the big meet tomorrow?" Dad asked.

The question took me by surprise. After the whole situation with the screams I heard, I forgot that I was heading into the most important meet of my life. "Yes," I answered. I tried not to sound fake or distracted, even though that's how I felt. I turned my focus to the meal. "This is delicious."

"How was school today?" Mom questioned.

"It was OK," I told her.

"Just OK?" Mom replied.

"I have a lot to worry about and, with this meet tomorrow, school work just isn't a priority. I'm trying to manage everything. My teachers are being cooperative though."

"That's good," she replied. "You'll do fine; you always do."

She always told me that. I could have the worse day in the world, tell her all about it, and she would say, "it'll be fine; it always is." I told my friends that it was my mom's motto.

"How was work?" I decided to reverse the roles.

"Big case," Dad said. "I think I'm going to be away for a week or two to work on the evidence." Dad was a high profile lawyer, which is where our fortune came from. He was a strict guy and always knew what he wanted but that's what helped him become so successful. Unfortunately, he could be a real jerk sometimes.

"Oh," I replied. It wasn't unusual for him to be away for work. When he was away, Mom was usually a wreck. She tried to lose herself in her work but she couldn't help but think that Dad was running around on her. I was never sure what I thought about it. He could have been but who knows.

Someone knocked on the back door in the corner of the kitchen. Dad answered it and found Grandpa Atlas on the other side. My dad's dad, Grandpa Atlas was the only grandparent I knew. The others passed away before I was born. A very tiny man, short and skinny with just enough gray hair to cover his small head, he looked every minute of his age.

"Dad, what're you doing here?" Dad questioned.

Mom signaled for Grandpa to come in. "Join us for dinner."

"Thank you, but I already ate," Grandpa said as he entered and sat down at the table. "I came to see Trey before his big meet tomorrow."

I smiled. He remembered. "How are you?"

"Oh, fine, fine. How are you?"

"I'm good. I'm ready for tomorrow."

His eyes told me he wasn't convinced. "I brought you a lucky charm." He pulled a small jewelry box out of his coat pocket and pushed it across the table at me.

"Dad, you shouldn't have," my dad said.

"Shush," Grandpa replied. "Go ahead, open it."

I opened the navy blue box. Inside, was a leather, braided necklace. The pendant on it was something I'd never seen before. It was diamond shaped but with a wing on each side. Silver in color, maybe pure silver—which I knew could be worth money. It was old and worn but appeared to have been cleaned up by a jeweler. A blue triangle-shaped gem sat in the top part of the diamond shape. I had no idea what it was but it had my interest.

"It's beautiful," Mom exclaimed. An old and worn necklace had to be intriguing to an archaeologist.

"Yeah," I agreed.

"Read the card," Grandpa told me.

I hadn't noticed the card—actually it was a piece of parchment—until Grandpa said that. "This ancient necklace is one of a kind and carries the destiny of specific individuals. Trey Atlas, you are the next person in line. Your possession of this necklace is a sign of royalty and it will bring you prosperity, peace, and good fortune."

"That must be a powerful little pendant," Dad chuckled.

"It sounds like if you wear it tomorrow, you'll win and go to nationals." Mom looked at me with hope.

"It will help," Grandpa said. "You will wear it, won't you?

"Of course," I told him. "I'm willing to try anything to get to nationals."

"Well you don't really need any help," Mom said, "but the necklace can't hurt.

I put the necklace on and Grandpa smiled from ear to ear. "Thank you," I said.

"You're very welcome," Grandpa said. "I just knew it belonged to you."

"Can I talk to you alone?" Dad asked Mom. He stood and went to the living room. Mom followed after him.

Grandpa looked at me with concern. "You sure you're alright?"

He knew something. "Fine."

"Trey, I know you're lying to me. I don't want to talk about it now, because your mom and dad will be back in any minute, but I know that today was not a normal day for you."

I tried to hide the surprise. "What do you mean?"

He leaned in closer. "I didn't write your name on the card that came with the necklace."

Butterflies grew in my stomach. "Wh...Who wrote my name...then?"

Mom and Dad came back into the kitchen and Grandpa turn-ed his attention to them. "Everything alright?"

"Yeah," Mom said as she and Dad took seats at the table again. Dad said nothing. Instead, he paged through the mail that he brought from the living room.

"I should be going," Grandpa stood up. "Good luck tomor-row, Trey. I'll await the news of your victory."

"Thanks." I went to see Grandpa out and opened the door. "And thank you for the necklace."

"You're welcome," he said. "I promise you that all will be revealed soon." He winked and walked away.

I closed the door. "I'm going to my room to do homework."

"Don't you want to talk about the necklace?" Mom asked. "Or the meet?"

"Nothing more to say and I have to get my homework done." I grabbed the box with the necklace from the table then practically ran up the steps and closed my door. I didn't want to talk about my day anymore. I needed processing time.

The waterbed rippled like my mind trying to figure out what Grandpa meant by 'everything would be revealed soon'. It was a very strange visit from Grandpa who I'd never known to be a strange person.

I closed my eyes and hoped to find sleep but the piercing scream echoed in my ears. It wasn't just the memory. It came from my waterbed. I knew it would be a long night with hardly any sleep. The scream was in the water.

A World Burning in the Pool

First thing the next morning, I entered the school. School was the last place most students wanted to be on a Saturday, especially so early, but I looked forward to it. Swimming was my passion and today was the most important day in my athletic career.

I headed toward the locker room. The necklace from Grandpa around my neck; the pendant tucked under my white "New York" shirt. I intended to use the necklace for luck like the card said I could.

"Trey," a girl's voice called to me before I entered the locker room.

Ashley walked toward me. She looked great. Her brown hair pulled back in a ponytail, her black skirt hugged her waist, and her shirt fit perfectly. If I had time for a serious girlfriend, she'd be the one. But since she was my other best friend, I was afraid of ruining our relationship.

"Hey Ash," I greeted her. We hugged, kissed quickly, and then I just looked at her. "You look great."

"You too," she said. There was a moment of awkwardness before she refocused. "Are you ready?"

I wanted to tell her that I'd hardly slept because I was so busy trying to drown out the screams. I had even put my iPod on and I could hear the screams over the music, probably because they were on my mind. I wanted to tell her that I was nervous about getting in the water because I knew I would hear the screams again. I wanted to tell her about the screams so that someone knew about them. I wanted to know if someone else could hear them, find out if I was hallucinating.

I wanted to tell her about Grandpa's visit, the necklace, and his strange messages that I couldn't get out of my head. I wanted her to know that I was going crazy inside and that I wasn't ready for the meet. But I also wanted everyone to continue to think of me as a cool and confident guy, even under pressure. After all, I knew it was one of the reasons so many girls found me intriguing.

So I lied. "Of course I'm ready, I was born ready for this day."

"I figured."

As expected, she bought my act. I'd sort of hoped she wouldn't. I needed to talk. I didn't want to be alone with this; I didn't like to be alone.

"Your eyes tell me something is bothering you," Ashley said. "What's wrong?" Her eyes stared into mine.

"Nothing," I answered. "I just have to go get ready."

She looked at me with doubt, fighting the urge to ask me again. "Trey, I'm your best friend. I know you better than anyone and I know something is bothering you. But, like usual, I'll walk away and we'll talk about his later. Good luck out there."

She walked a few paces away and then turned. "You know, your relationships with us girls would be so much easier if you didn't try to hide things from us." I watched her walk away until she turned the corner to go to the pool. That's the thing; I didn't really have relationships with girls. I just had dates.

I pushed my conversation with Ashley out of my mind and went into the locker room. I changed into my swim gear, ran my hair under the water for a few minutes, and then met my teammates on the bench near the pool. The bleachers around the pool were filling up. The fairly new pool had enough bleachers to fit everyone comfortably.

"This is it, Trey," Kyle leaned forward to look at me, past the rest of the team.

"We're ready to take the region by storm," I told him.

"You're going to take the region by storm," he corrected. "Not 'we'."

That reminded me of the luck that was supposed to be granted to me by the necklace. And then I realized that I took the necklace off when I changed and I didn't put it back on. I got up and hurried into the locker room. I found the necklace in my boot in the locker. I took it out and put it around my neck and then headed back to the bench.

A referee took a microphone and smacked his hand on it to make sure it was working. "Ladies and Gentlemen we will now start our tournament. The winning individuals will go to regionals."

I looked into the crowd, searching for Ashley, my parents, and Coal. I found them, and just as suspected, they sat together. My parents were talking, possibly arguing. Dad looked like a gray hair was appearing every minute. Mom seemed to add a wrinkle to her face just as quickly. Their marriage wasn't easy, with all of the stress and Dad's travel but I hated that they argued in front of Ashley and Coal. Why couldn't they keep it private?

"Treyton Atlas," the referee called me. He apparently chose to use my full name even though I always made clear, so did Coach, that I wanted to be called Trey.

I walked to the block assigned to me. I saw the starter; he would tell us when to begin. There was a turn, stroke, and finish judge. And the timekeepers with the stopwatches were trained, unbiased, high school students.

I climbed up onto the block. First up, the freestyle competition, one of my favorites. "Swimmers ready," the starter called. I got into position. "Three," the starter counted down, "two, one, go!"

I dove into the pool and swam as fast as I could. I needed to do four laps, down and back, to get the victory. As I turned and started back to the starting line, a light from the water caught my eye but I didn't let myself lose focus. I swam my laps, made it to the finish before everyone else.

The crowd cheered as the referee raised my hand. The light, still shining, distracted me. It came from my chest, from the blue gem on my necklace. Did anyone else see it? Maybe I really did go crazy.

The referee finished telling Coach my times, she congratulated

me, and I went back to the bench and wrapped myself in a towel. I looked at the necklace, moving it between my fingers to figure out what was going on. No one else seemed to notice the light. Something was written on the necklace; something that wasn't there before.

I quickly ran to the bleachers, even though Coach wouldn't normally let me do that.

"Congrats, Trey," Coal said. Ashley said the same. I didn't answer. I was on a mission and I needed to act fast.

"What's wrong?" Mom asked.

I grabbed Mom's camera, took my necklace off and snapped a picture. The necklace didn't have as much light and lettering as I saw just a few minutes ago but it would still be proof of what happened to the necklace.

My mom looked at me like I was crazy and I told her I would explain after the meet. I handed her the camera, put the necklace back on, and then went back to the bench.

As I sat on the bench, waiting for my next competition, I thought about the light and lettering on the necklace. I looked at the necklace now and found that it looked like it did when I first took it out of the box. No light coming from the gem; no lettering on the silver.

I got so caught up in the strange happenings of the necklace that I didn't even acknowledge my teammates when they congratulated me for winning. I'd also been so distracted that I didn't realize, at least until now, that there was no screaming in the water today. Now my mind raced with that thought. Why wouldn't there be screaming today?

Maybe I wasn't hallucinating today. That was a stupid thought. I saw lights and letters appear on a necklace and then disappear a few minutes later. I couldn't explain what happened and I didn't have time to care.

"Treyton Atlas," the official called my name for the next competition. This one was the butterfly, fly for short, my least favorite stroke. In my opinion, it was the hardest to perfect. I walked, concentrating on doing my best in the fly, to the block. I climbed up and took a deep breath. The water below shimmered in the sunlight that came through the big glass windows behind the bleachers.

"On the mark," the starter shouted. "Three, two, one, go!" I dove into the pool and set my mind on the technique. Judges watched from the sides of the pool to make sure the swimmers didn't cheat or make mistakes. I didn't want this one to cost me my chance at regionals.

I was focused and determined to win until I saw the flames. FIRE!

Fire in the pool. FIRE IN THE WATER! I stopped swimming, stuck my head up and yelled, "FIRE!" as loud as I could. The other swimmers stopped and looked at me. "Fire," I yelled again. Everyone started screaming and looking around. But no one saw fire.

I looked down in the water and didn't see any flames, just the diminishing light from my necklace. I dove under and watched, as the light from my necklace grew stronger. It seemed to diffuse through the whole pool, growing in intensity the longer I stayed under.

I took my necklace off and held it in my hand. I swam to the surface, keeping the necklace under the water, and stuck my head out to breathe. Everyone watched me. They probably thought I had gone crazy, but I dove back down anyway. As I swam to the bottom of the pool, I saw the fire again.

In fact, I saw a building on fire. An ancient building, looked like Greek architecture. I heard the woman's blood-curdling scream again. Her black hair was a mess and her dark gray robes were torn and soaked. Who was she? Why was she screaming? Then I saw them; the sources of her trouble. Ninjas, dressed in navy blue, approached her.

I needed air, so I swam back to the surface, slowly. As I moved away from the bottom of the pool, the picture grew more distant. It was like an airplane at takeoff. And before I knew it, I saw an entire island. I shot out of the water, but I kept my hand with the necklace in the water, and gasped for a breath. I took a couple deep breaths, then held one, and dove under again.

My vision refocused on the girl. Ninjas surrounded her. What island was I looking at? Who was the girl? Who were the ninjas? Why was I seeing this in the pool?

I swam to the very bottom of the pool and put my face against the floor. I stared into the dark eyes of the brown haired girl. Swords at her throat, she didn't seem afraid. Her young face was scratched and dirty. She was around my age.

She stared right into my eyes. Her eyes begged me for help. I, for the first time in a long time, felt helpless. I didn't know what I could do about the situation I watched. I didn't even know where she was. And I knew that once I got to the surface, people would be questioning me like I was crazy.

Surface. I didn't take a breath in minutes. I could hold my breath for a long time but this was a new record. I didn't even feel like I needed air. The light from the necklace seemed to provide oxygen to my cells.

The girl spoke. "Help me. My world needs your help, young prince." I couldn't believe what I heard. Was she talking to me? Did she see me like I saw her? Young prince? Maybe it wasn't me she was referring too. But she was looking right at me. She had to be in an English speaking country.

Kyle came up beside me, grabbed my body and pulled me to the surface. He carried me to the side of the pool and pushed me up onto the floor. He hopped up and leaned over to give me CPR.

"I'm fine," I told him, pushing him away. "I'm fine."

"You were under the water really long," he replied.

I sat up. "But I'm fine."

Kyle looked at me in awe, "But..." He didn't know what to say. He expected that I would be unconscious and here I was, saying I was alright.

"Look, I'm sorry you didn't get a chance to kiss me but I'm actually alright."

"Shut up! You're freakin' gross. I was going to save your life..."

"Chill out, dude," I cut him off. "I was only joking."

"So what happened?" he asked, calming down. "What was all the screaming about fire for?"

"Did you see it?" I asked him. "Did you hear her cries?"

Mom, Dad, Ashley, Coal and Coach all came over to me to make sure I was alright and interrupted Kyle before he could answer me. I assured them I was fine and that I didn't have the problem.

"What's the problem then?" Coach asked me. "Where was the fire?"

I looked at my necklace, the letters just about faded away and the last bit of light diminished. I knew the next statement would make them mark me as delusional but I said it anyway. "There was a world burning in the pool."

See the Key, Young Prince

Coach, Mom, and Dad insisted that I see a doctor right away. Dad drove me right to the hospital emergency room. Mom took Coal and Ashley home. They were supposed to go home with me, but plans changed. Mom said she would meet us at the hospital as soon as she could. Speaking of plans changing, I had to forfeit the competition. My dream about regionals and nationals was dead and gone.

The receptionist in the emergency room looked at Dad with exhausted eyes. The waiting room was packed with people with everything from broken limbs to horrible coughs. I sat down in a chair and waited for Dad to finish with the receptionist. I didn't want to stand there while he explained how I was delusional. That would have been embarrassing.

Dad made it over to me and sat down. He didn't say anything, just stared into space. I couldn't help but think that I let everyone down.

Everyone had counted on me to take the school to nationals. Everyone thought I was the best thing to ever happen to our high school. But now I embarrassed the school in front of numerous other schools by rambling about a world on fire in the pool. I couldn't help it; it's not like I wanted to believe it either. But I saw and heard everything myself. Even if I did exaggerate since it was only a building and not a world on fire.

"I need to ask you something," Dad said. "It's not easy for me and it won't be easy for you, but I need the truth. I need the truth before the doctor evaluates you because I prefer to hear it from you first."

I looked at him with concern. I was pretty sure I knew what question he was going to ask me but I couldn't believe we had gotten to that point. I nodded to tell him to go ahead and ask the question.

"Did you take any drugs?" he asked. The exact question I'd expected.

"No," I told him quickly. I had never taken drugs. I was too health conscience to even think about it. It would ruin all of my hard work.

"Could anyone have slipped you a drug?" Dad questioned.

That scenario was certainly more likely but I knew for a fact that it didn't happen. "No."

We spent the next half hour, until Mom showed up, sitting in silence. I stared into space, thinking about all that took place and how my hard work was ruined. When Mom came in to the emergency room, she sat next to me. She questioned me just like Dad. I told her that I didn't do drugs; no one slipped me drugs, and that I was fine.

"I'm going to use the bathroom," I said. I wanted to get away from the third degree and I wanted to test out a theory I had about my necklace. I stretched and then walked to the bathroom. Once in the bathroom, with the door locked, I went to the sink and turned on the water. I ran the necklace under water and it started to emit light from the blue gem. Letters began to appear. They weren't English letters but they looked semi-familiar.

The longer I held the necklace under the water, the more distinct the letters became and the more intense the light grew. An image appeared in the water stream; it was the woman again.

"Help us, young prince," she called. "Please, I beg you. If you hear me, you must help us."

"I'm trying," I answered.

A knock on the bathroom door interrupted the connection. "Trey," Dad called, "the doctor will see you now."

I pulled the necklace out from under the water, turned the faucet, and put the necklace back around my neck. I dried the pendant with a paper towel until the light and letters disappeared. "Trey," Dad called again.

"I'll be right out," I replied. My theory that the necklace was the cause of the whole scene was true. How would I explain that to Mom and Dad and the doctor without sounding like someone who should be carried away by the white coats?

The doctor checked my eyes and ears and asked me questions about what happened. She took blood to do some tests. Then she told Mom and Dad that she didn't think drugs were involved and that I didn't seem to have any illness symptoms. Her explanation was that I was making the whole story up for attention.

Obviously she didn't know me or she would have realized that

I didn't need attention. The whole school was focused on my attempt to get to nationals. I didn't tell her that though. I figured she would say that the story was a way for me to get rid of the pressure. The doctor told my mom and dad that she would call when the results of the blood tests came in but that we could go home. She told me to get some sleep.

The drive home was quieter than expected. I thought both of my parents would out compete each other to lecture me but neither one even tried. They told me to let them know if I needed to talk and that I shouldn't let the pressure of the school get to me. They said I just needed to do my best. We stopped at McDonald's drive-thru for some food. We were all hungry because we didn't eat anything since breakfast and it was already late afternoon.

I gobbled down my cheeseburger, realizing that I would have to work twice as hard to burn it off. I told Dad to drop me off at the gym so I could work out. Surprisingly, he did and then they headed home. I guess they figured I needed to have a normal part of my day.

I did my usual routine as quickly as I could and then ran home. I had some things on my mind about the world in the pool and I wanted to do some research so I could get those answers.

After my shower, I got Mom's camera and hooked it up to my computer. I searched through and downloaded the picture I took at the pool.

It wasn't what I expected. I took a picture of the pendant when it was still emitting light and some letters were still there. That's not what the picture showed. No light. No letters. The proof I counted on didn't show up in the picture.

I had to run the pendant under the water and find out what the letters looked like so I could write them on a piece of paper. That way, I could find out what was written on it.

I took the necklace to the bathroom, filled up a bucket that was under the sink, and dropped the necklace in. The blue gem started to emit light that intensified slowly. The light created the image of the city in the water. I observed the image carefully, taking in the details.

I ran back to my room and took a piece of paper from my desk. Taking it to the sink in the bathroom, I described what the city looked like.

The architecture seemed to be a mixture of ancient Greek and modern skyscrapers. Some of the buildings resembled the Capitol Building in Washington. Most were made up of marble, with silver and gold, among other metals I didn't recognize. Rivers ran between buildings, and even right under some buildings. Smoke came from the center of the city. Three large rings of water circled the center where the fire burned.

The young woman knelt at a pond outside a large marble building. A fire burned out of control behind her. A palace? A temple? Her black hair matted; her face covered in scratches and dirt. Her white robes torn. The image was the same way it was in the pool earlier that afternoon. A repeat?

No screams or calls for help. She was just there. She looked terrified. I wanted to help her but I didn't even know what city I was looking at. She must have heard my thoughts because she said, "See the key, young Prince. Please hurry."

I pulled the necklace out of the bucket, cutting off the vision, and observed the letters. I quickly wrote them down before they disappeared.

I headed downstairs with the necklace and paper. I figured Mom would be able to help me interpret what I saw in the water. She sat at the kitchen table writing out checks to pay our bills.

"Mom," I interrupted, " do you have a few minutes to talk?"

She looked at me. Most other days she probably would have said to wait until she finished but she signaled me to sit down.

"What's up?" she asked.

"I want to talk about what I saw in the pool today," I told her. "The burning world, actually only one building was on fire, came from light emitted from the necklace Grandpa gave me. I think it's enchanted or something."

"Don't be ridiculous," she replied. "It's an ordinary necklace. You're just really stressed."

"Mom," I cut her off. "I'm telling you, I know what I saw. When I put the necklace under water it emits light from the blue gem and then the world appears. A building is burning and a woman is calling for help, my help I think. She is calling me a young prince."

My mom looked at me with disbelief. She thought I was making this up. How could I convince her? "Here," I pushed the paper to her, "look at that."

She read what I wrote and then looked up at me. "That's vivid," she said.

"I saw it as if I was standing right in front of it."

"Those letters," she pointed to the letters I copied from the necklace pendant. "What do they mean?"

"I was hoping you would tell me."

"So you don't know?"

"No." I looked at her. Her eyes told me she knew something about the world, the letters, and my whole story.

"It's Atlantis," she said. "These letters here say 'Atlantis'. How did you know to write that?"

"They were on my necklace."

She gasped. "Your necklace? The one from Grandpa?"

"Yes! Mom, that's what I'm telling you." It sounded like she finally got it. "But how do you know it says Atlantis?"

"Trey, I study ancient artifacts for a living. I read all types of ancient languages on a daily basis. I've seen this language before, though I can't remember what language it is."

I looked at her, trying to read her expression. Was she holding something from me? I had a feeling she was.

"Do you know what Atlantis is?" Mom asked.

"It's an island said to be lost. But it's a myth."

"Correct," she responded. I could see there was more.

"So why does this necklace say Atlantis on it? Why am I seeing Atlantis in the water?"

"Maybe you're not seeing Atlantis," Mom told me. "And maybe the necklace is left over from the Greeks. I don't know. I'm thinking that you shouldn't wear it anymore. In fact, you should get rid of it."

"But..." I looked at her with concern. "Grandpa gave it to me." The fact that she wanted to get rid of it just because I had visions, visions she thought I made up, shocked me.

"Give it to me," Mom said again, this time with more seriousness.

"Shouldn't we give it back to Grandpa?"

"No," she answered, "just give it to me."

I handed her the necklace and watched as she threw it in the garbage.

"Now we'll be done with this," she told me.

I nodded. I was glad to get rid of the necklace that ruined my chances at nationals. But at the same time, curiosity tore at my soul. I wanted to know more about it. I needed to know more about it.

"That's all," Mom said.

In her mind it was over but I wasn't done trying to under- stand what the visions meant. And I knew just the person to see.

A History Lesson From Grandpa Atlas

Obviously Grandpa Atlas was the best person to talk to about the visions. Beyond the fact that he gave me the necklace, he loved mythology and was considered an expert in Greek and Roman mythology. He probably knew enough about Atlantis to help me out. At least I hoped he did. I told my mom I was going to visit him and left.

Grandpa lived about a half mile from my house so it wasn't far to walk. My cell phone rang as I approached the halfway point of my walk and the screen showed me Coal's name.

"What's up?" I asked him.

"I wanted to see what you were up to. I was worried about you after the incident at the meet today."

"I'm fine."

"What did the doctor say?"

"She said that it wasn't drugs and I didn't seem to have any medical issues. They took blood to do some tests but she told me to go home and sleep. She suggested that I made it up because I needed attention."

Coal chuckled at that thought. "You? Need attention?"

"That's what I thought too."

"So what's going on?"

"I don't know. I'm not making this up. There really was a city in the water and a building on fire. I proved it at home by putting my necklace, the new one I got from Grandpa, in water. The vision appeared. There's a girl calling for help."

"And where's this city?" Coal questioned.

"Mom told me the letters that show up on the jewel, when it's wet, spell out Atlantis. I'm thinking that the visions might be of Atlantis."

"But Atlantis is a myth? Why are you having visions about a mythical city and a woman calling you for help?"

"I don't know but I intend to find out. I have to prove that I'm not seeing and hearing things and that I'm not making things up to get attention. Plus, I feel like I need to help this girl, whoever and wherever she is."

"How are you going to find out?"

"I'm going to see Grandpa Atlas. He gave me the necklace so if anyone can help me, he's the one."

"That's kinda strange, don't you think?"

"What is?"

"Grandpa Atlas, who's an expert on mythology, gave you a necklace for good luck. Now you're seeing a city being destroyed and hearing the screams of a woman you never met. And on top of that, your mom, who's an archaeologist, can read the language on the necklace. She gives you information that makes you believe the city is Atlantis. Is this all a big coincidence?"

I thought about what he was suggesting. Was all of this really a coincidence or was something else going on? I didn't think of it until Coal suggested it. Of course, no one knew about the fact that I heard the woman screaming prior to receiving the necklace. If I told them that, the focus would be off the necklace and on my sanity.

"Well, my mom threw the necklace away so I guess I don't have to worry about it."

"Dude, that could've been worth money."

I left an awkward silence. I didn't care about the monetary value of the necklace. But Coal did; that necklace could have been worth enough for his family to live off the rest of their lives. But money wasn't that big an issue with me. I never wanted for anything.

"Listen," I said, "I'm just about at the house. I need to talk to him. I'll call you later."

"Sounds good. Later."

"Bye." I hung up the phone and walked up the steps to my grandfather's porch. I knocked on the door and waited.

"Thank goodness you're here," Grandpa Atlas said as soon as he opened the door. "Hurry, come in."

Grandpa was old fashioned. He kept Greek and Roman artifacts that Mom brought home to him scattered around his house. I always figured that Grandpa Atlas loved mom for her love of archeology. In fact, he treated mom better than he treated his own son.

He led me to the kitchen and told me to sit down. His kitchen was small and old. "So tell me about it," Grandpa said. I could

tell he was anxious about something.

"About what?"

"The visions of course."

I didn't realize he knew about them. I guess Mom or Dad called him. His eyes begged me to fill him in. They told me he could help, if he just understood. So I filled him in. I told him about the screams I first heard. I trusted Grandpa more than anyone and I knew he wouldn't think I was insane. Besides, I had reasons to believe he already knew about the screams from things he said the day before. Then I told him about the visions in the pool that seemed to be generated by the light emitted from the gem on the necklace.

"Tell me more about the city," he said. "What did it look like?"

I described the buildings as ancient Greek architecture mixed with modern skyscrapers. I told him that there were canals running through the city like streets, along with streets made out of stone. I told him that there seemed to be an elevated plateau or hill with buildings on top. One of the buildings burned out of control.

"What did the building that was on fire look like?"

I thought about it. "I'm not sure; I didn't see it in detail. I just saw a lot of smoke. I know it looked like marble and that it was the color of..." I couldn't think of anything better so I said "...sand."

"Was the whole land an island?" he questioned.

"Yes." I knew for a fact that it was because I remembered seeing the distant view from the top of the pool. I could see the land surrounded by water.

Grandpa was silent for a time. I could tell he was deep in thought. Something was bothering him; he knew something and he was debating whether or not he should tell me. I let him sit in silence so he could think.

Finally he said, "You saw Atlantis." He paused to watch my reaction. "Your mom and dad wouldn't want me to tell you what I am going to tell you, but I think it's important considering the visions you're having. Atlantis is real."

"Real? But I thought it's a myth? I thought it was lost?"

"No, no, no," Grandpa said. "Trey, Atlantis is real. It isn't lost. It just got hidden from the world. It's flourishing on its own."

"How? Why? Where?" I had so many questions.

"Atlantis is over sixty-thousand years old. And for about forty-five thousand years, it was the most successful civilization in the world. But then the Atlantean royalty became greedy. They wanted to conquer other countries and take over the world. Things went wrong and Atlantis' king had the island hidden from the world.

"Atlantis disappeared from the world map about eleven thousand years ago. But Trey, it's not really gone. It's still there. Though it sounds like the Atlanteans need help and they're calling on you."

"So Atlantis is real, it exists, and is hidden from the world. And now, for some reason, a young woman, presumably from Atlantis, is calling me for help." I stopped, unsure of the whole story. How could it be true? I didn't want to believe it but Grandpa sounded so sure. It was all so strange.

"It's not all that surprising," Grandpa said. I couldn't believe he said that. I was in shock and he didn't think it was all that surprising. "Can you describe the young woman?" Grandpa asked. "I need to know if it's who I think it is.

I tried to picture her. "She's young, maybe a little older than me. She's beautiful, even though her face was scratched and covered in dirt. She has black hair."

"What about her eyes? What did her eyes look like?"

I concentrated, recreating the vision in my head. I saw the young woman again. But I couldn't see what her eyes looked like. "I know they were dark," I told him. "But I didn't take notice to her eye color. It feels like the color was hidden from me, even though I looked right into them."

"Aerian," he exclaimed. "It's exactly what I feared. Trey, there's something happening in Atlantis."

"Wait, what's Aerian?"

"That's the woman's name. She's in trouble."

"Hence the reason she was cut and her clothes torn."

"Someone, or something, took her power," Grandpa explained.

"Her power?"

"She's a sorceress."

He knew too much. "You know all of this about my visions and you don't think it's surprising. What aren't you telling me?"

He reached his hand out, "Let me see the necklace."

"Mom threw it out," I told him. "She said it wasn't worth the problems."

"Then what's around your neck?"

I grabbed the leather strip that hung around my neck. The necklace was back. How? I watched Mom throw it away. I took it off and handed the necklace to Grandpa.

"Trey, this is a necklace from Atlantean royalty. Whoever holds this necklace is very highly regarded in the Atlantean society. They are even crowned King."

I stared at him. My stomach had butterflies. "Y-you gave me a royal necklace from Atlantis?"

"Yes," Grandpa answered. "This necklace would make you King."

"How did you get it?"

"Doesn't matter. It's yours now."

"But Mom threw it in the garbage. It can't be here."

"Once this necklace attaches to someone with Atlantean royal blood, it never leaves. It will always return."

I couldn't believe what I was hearing. "How do you know so... Wait...Royal blood?"

"Trey, your mom and dad asked me to never share this with you but I don't have a choice. The revolution that threatens the island of Atlantis is starting and you're the only one that can stop it."

"This is insane," I stood up from the table. "I have to go."

"Trey, you have to go to Atlantis and find out why Aerian is calling you."

"No way!" I said.

"You have to," he reiterated. "There is no choice here. If you don't go, and Aerian dies, the future of Atlantis is bleak."

"I have too much going for me here to worry about an island that has nothing to do with me," I told him.

"Did you listen to me?" he was upset. "I just told you that you're an Atlantean king. You're empire is in trouble and thousands of people are going to die if you don't do something."

"I don't care about thousands of people I never met. And I don't care about a legacy I've never been a part of. My life is fine the way it is."

"Trey, you're part of Atlantis, whether you like it or not."

"I'm leaving." I turned to go.

Grandpa put his hand on my shoulder to stop me. "Where's the necklace?"

I thought about it. I gave it to him and he didn't give it back. "You have it."

"Not anymore." He looked at my neck and I followed his eyes. The necklace was back around my neck. "Trey, that necklace is not going away. It ruined your chances at nationals but that's only the beginning. Sooner or later, whoever is attacking Atlantis is going to find out that you have the necklace. They're going to realize that you're an Atlantean royal. If you don't go to them, they're going to come to you."

A dagger went through my heart. The necklace marked me as Atlantean royalty and I couldn't get rid of it. "Then why did you give it to me? It's ruining my life!" I tried to contain my anger.

"Trey," Grandpa said with softness in his voice, "you have an obligation. You may not like it but you're needed to save Atlantis. Can you be responsible for the death of thousands of people? Can you ignore your legacy and let it be lost forever? Can you force an evil to come into our world to find you?" He paused.

I choked back tears and fought to whisper. "Why did you give me the necklace? Why won't you tell me?"

"This is bigger than me, Trey," Grandpa said. "This is your legacy. It's your destiny and you can't deny that."

"I'm going home," I started to leave.

"Good idea," Grandpa yelled after me. "I'll be there soon and we'll talk again."

THE TRUTH HURTS

Twenty minutes had passed since I got home from Grandpa Atlas' house. My life was in total chaos. Grandpa sat at the kitchen table with Mom and Dad. They all stared at me as I stopped at the bottom of the steps.

Grandpa smiled with enthusiasm. Dad looked frustrated and annoyed. Mom seemed to be on the verge of tears. She knew that I was struggling with the whole situation of the visions and I'm sure Grandpa filled them in on our conversation.

"Everything happens for a reason," Mom's voice quivered. "There's a reason this necklace gave you visions of Atlantis."

"Stop it," Dad reprimanded her. "Those visions are just daydreams. How can you sit here and say that this is meant to be?"

Mom shot him a look of anger. "We've been through this."

"And I told you that I don't think he should go."

"I didn't say I was going," I informed them.

"And I told you that he has no choice," Mom ignored my statement. "How can he live with himself, or us, if he stays here and thousands of people are murdered?"

"They won't be murdered because Atlantis doesn't exist," Dad yelled, now thoroughly angry.

"It does exist," Grandpa Atlas jumped into the argument. "And you know it deep down. Maybe you should put your work aside for a moment and actually think about your son."

"Maybe you should stop putting crazy stories in my son's head," Dad yelled back.

"Maybe you should remember the agreement!" Grandpa spat.

His words lit up my mind. "What agreement?"

"That's enough," Mom cut it off. "Arguing about this doesn't help anyone. Trey needs to decide what he's going to do."

"What agreement?" I tried again.

"Never mind," Grandpa said, "it doesn't matter."

"It does matter," I said sternly. "This is my life we're talking

about. Everything about my life changed over night and now I'm supposed to save an entire island civilization. With everything that's happening, there can't be any secrets. The more I know the better off I'll be. So stop hiding this stuff from me and tell me the truth!"

"Sometimes the truth hurts, Trey," Grandpa said.

"This whole thing hurts," I told him. "You don't think I can handle another secret?"

"I'll tell him," Mom jumped in.

"No you won't!" Dad yelled. "We agreed."

"Tell me what?" I asked.

"Trey, sit down," Grandpa instructed.

"You will not tell him," Dad yelled even louder. "I won't allow it."

I sat down at the table across from Grandpa. I was anxious to hear the secret but not sure I should since it made Dad so upset.

"You're ruining his life," Dad directed his anger at Grandpa. "This is your fault! You promised he would live a normal life."

"I promised I would do what I could to provide him with a normal life," Grandpa told him. "I can't control this."

"What do you mean you promised to provide me a normal life? Why would you have to make that promise?"

"Trey," Mom's voice was soft with concern, "There's some-thing we hid from you. We hid it to protect you but we can't hide it anymore."

Dad interrupted, "I can't believe your doing this." He walked out of the kitchen toward the living room.

Mom watched him leave and then turned back to me. "Trey," Mom paused for a moment as if to think of how to say what she had to say and then continued. "Trey, you're adopted."

Adopted. The word sank in to my brain. Why would they hide that from me? I wanted to ask out loud but the words wouldn't form.

Mom waited for a few moments but then continued. "You were brought to us by Grandpa."

"I'm not really your Grandfather," Grandpa Atlas said. "I'm actually a royal sorcerer from Atlantis. It was my job to get you off the island of Atlantis and somewhere safe."

"Wha...Why?...What?" I stumbled to find words.

Grandpa Atlas, who now wasn't really my grandfather, tried to explain. "I told you a little about this when we were in my kitchen but I wanted your parents with us when I told you the rest. You're an Atlantean royal. Sixteen years ago, when you were just a few days old, your family gave me the job to protect you and find a place where you could live safely until you were needed. I brought you here and made an agreement with your parents...uh, adopted parents. They were unable to have a child of their own so they agreed to raise you and in return they were blessed with an Atlantean spell for a prosperous life. That's why your family has so much money and your family life has been so good."

"I'm so confused," I said.

"You're an Atlantean," Mom reiterated what Grandpa told me. "We raised you until..."

"...Until what?" I cut her off.

"Trey," Grandpa took over again, "There's a prophecy that calls for you to lead the island of Atlantis. Your family was afraid you would be killed before your time came."

"Why?"

"The Knights of the Abyss, a group that has been trying to gain control of Atlantis for thousands of years, knows of your existence and they know that if you get in their way they will lose their chance to rule the island. But you're of age now and something very bad is happening in Atlantis. Your time is now."

"So you lied to me! You pretended I was your son and now..."

"You are our son," Mom cut me off.

"Now you're telling me that I'm a ruler of a world that doesn't exist..."

"It does exist," Grandpa reminded me.

"And there's a prophecy that sets my destiny to save the island, an island I have no recollection of ever being on, and lead it into the future."

"So you do understand," Grandpa had a hint of excitement in his voice.

"My life's in danger because the group destroying Atlantis knows I exist. This is all too much for me to take in. Just twenty-four hours ago, I was a normal sixteen-year-old and my biggest concern was whether or not I would win the swim meet and which girl I would date next. Now I'm orphaned and I'm supposed to take on the responsibility of saving and ruling an island. How am I supposed to do that?"

"You're not orphaned," Mom told me. "We love you. Nothing changed. The only difference is now you know that we're not related by blood. That doesn't mean that we're not family."

Grandpa nodded his head in agreement. "She's right. Nothing changed. And you have the blood of an Atlantean royal so you'll have no problem ruling the island..."

"Nothing changed!" I could feel the redness of anger in my face. "Nothing changed! Are you people oblivious to the world? The life I knew was ripped out from under me and I'm being forced to take on a new role and you sit here and say 'nothing changed'." I screamed as loud as I could, venting all of the frustration and anger and then stormed out of the house, slamming the kitchen door behind me.

From Pool to Pond

Unknown Location, Atlantis

Dark, cold, and dripping with water, the cave smelled stale. Man-made during the industrial revolution in Atlantis, the area was mined for coal, hydrome, and other important minerals from the Atlantean underground. About sixteen hundred feet from the entrance, the cavern split into two separate chambers. Two guards, their entire bodies wrapped in navy blue cloth, save for their eyes, guarded the left chamber. A silver wave on their headpiece symbolized the Knights of the Abyss.

A woman, dressed in robes like coal with a ponytail of the same color, approached and the two Knights moved to the side. They bowed to her as she walked between them and into the chamber. The silver in her eyes flickered with the light of the torches that burned in the center of the room. A tall, muscular Knight stood in the center of the room near one of the torches. Like the guards, he was dressed in navy blue. She stopped in front of him, bowed ever so slightly, and then waited.

"It's been too long, Jocasta," the man said.

"Surely you understand why, Cadmus?" Jocasta replied.

"Indeed," Cadmus said. "Sixteen years was the time needed for the plan to come to fruition."

"So why is it that you called me here?" Jocasta questioned.

"Our leader requests your services," Cadmus told her.

"So why did he send you then?"

"His time is coming. But for now, he has entrusted me to ensure the survival of the Knights of the Abyss. His only request was that I call on you for guidance."

"He always was a smart man." Jocasta laughed without chang-ing her expression.

"He didn't give me reasons that I should call on you but I never question his judgment."

"Obviously or you wouldn't be standing here." Jocasta swiped the room with her mercury eyes. "So what is it that I can do for you?"

"As you know, the Knights of the Abyss were founded on a

hatred for all that is Atlantis. We spent hundreds of years preparing to wipe this civilization from the map, just like Aruc made the world think happened eleven thousand years ago..."

Jocasta interrupted him with a hiss. "Skip the story session. I already know all about the Knights of the Abyss and I know about the plan. I was part of this plan since the very beginning. What is it that they want me to do now?"

The silver wave on Cadmus' headpiece bounced candlelight onto the cave walls. "We infiltrated the palace and exterminated the royal family."

Jocasta perked up. "Did you find the boy?"

"That's why I called you here," Cadmus replied.

"Please tell me he wasn't killed."

"No," Cadmus grew annoyed. "It's worse than that."

"How could it be worse than him being murdered?"

"He wasn't in the palace."

Jocasta scoffed. "He had to be."

"He wasn't. We still have control of the palace and we searched for him over a dozen times. He's not there."

"Did he escape during the attack?"

"Impossible," Cadmus told her. "We had the royal grounds completely surrounded.

"So where is he then?" Jocasta turned and stared at one of the torch's dancing flames.

"Now you understand why we called you," Cadmus said.

"You want me to locate the boy," Jocasta said.

"Precisely. Can you find him?"

"Take me to a pool of water and his location will be revealed."

Miami

The plastic bench was cool on the skin of my thighs. The navy and white swimsuit wasn't the most comfortable thing to wear to sit around, but I didn't plan to sit long. I needed to swim. Moonlight danced on the walls around me in a hypnotic fashion. I felt calmer all of a sudden, as if all of my worries were gone. It was normal for me to relax when I was at the pool.

"You okay, dear?" a soft, old voice asked. "You're usually swimming when you're in here." The old woman stood with a mop. I needed to answer her; she was the one that let me in to the pool at night whenever I wanted to swim. I owed her an answer but I wasn't going to tell her the truth.

"Just needed a moment to think," I told her. "I'm going in soon."

"Alright," she said, "I'll be in the gym if you need anything." Lizzy, the snow-haired janitor that worked nights in the gym and pool area, and I had built an understanding over the last few years. She knew I needed to practice at night and I ensured her that I wouldn't cause any problems. I even helped her clean her area of the school every so often as a thank you. She probably appreciated the company since it was lonely in the building at night. Plus, she didn't have any children so I think she thought of me as the son she never had. It was like she adopted me.

Adopted. There was that word again. I was adopted, though not by Lizzy. The two people I had accepted as my parents adopted me. Technically, they were my parents. They were the ones who raised me, cared for me, and made sure I grew up to become a productive member of society. But they weren't my parents. At least not in the way I had thought for sixteen years. They weren't my biological parents.

Nothing changed. Everything had changed. There's a special connection between a child and its mother and father. To not know who my real mother and father were was devastating. I knew it wasn't fair to my adopted parents. They raised me and treated me as though I was really theirs. But that connection was gone now. Now I didn't know who my parents were.

The emptiness inside me ached to find my real parents. But Grandpa.... the Sorcerer.... said I was from Atlantis. A member of the royal family sent away so that I would be protected. But that protection wasn't good enough anymore. *You're of age now and something very bad is happening in Atlantis. Your time is now.* If I wanted to find out who my real parents were, I'd have to go to Atlantis. And I'd have to save Atlantis or my real parents might get killed before I even met them. Even though I spent sixteen years of my life in Miami, and I didn't remember anything about Atlantis, the city outside the school windows suddenly felt foreign to me.

I stood up and walked to the edge of the pool. The shimmering liquid inches from my feet was all that felt natural to me now. I jumped in and started swimming laps.

Jocasta swiped her hand across the water. "Mnemosunero antigrafo." Ripples started in the center of the cavern lake and moved toward the edge, coming to a stop right at Jocasta's feet. The ripples continued for a few moments and then the surface settled instantly, like a bed sheet being stretched for smoothness.

The sorceress knelt on the bank of the lake and dipped her hand in the water without causing any disruption to the pond. The liquid remained still as she slowly swirled her hand and concentrated.

"I found the jewel," Jocasta told Cadmus. "I will try to follow it to the boy. Be ready to retrieve him." Cadmus stepped to the edge of the lake.

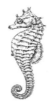

The water below me illuminated with the light from my necklace and the image of a cave appeared. I was getting accustomed to seeing the images in the water but this one was different than all of the previous ones. No scream. No girl in trouble. Just a cave below me. I swam to the surface and looked down where the cave was. I was farther away and it was like a movie in wide screen.

Something or someone moved on the very edge of the image. I focused on the movement and then swam toward it. A woman, dressed in black stood on the edge of the lake with a man dressed in a navy blue ninjas outfit .

Navy blue ninjas. Navy blue ninjas threatened the girl in my visions. Grand...well he, the sorcerer, said her name was Aerian. But this woman wasn't Aerian. And she didn't seem threatened by the ninja. So what exactly were they doing at a lake in a cave?

Back at the surface, I took a breath. I needed to figure my life out. I was a royal from Atlantis, an island that I thought was a myth just the other day. Now Atlantis needed my help and I was having all of these strange visions, which had to be connected to Atlantis.

What was the best way to straighten everything out? Should I ignore it? Should I discuss it with my fake family? Should I try to go to Atlantis and complete my destiny? That would probably be the best way to find out about my real family. Did I even want to know my real parents anyway? Sure it was an instinct to want to meet them but they're strangers to me. They chose to send me away for a reason. For protection. Well they screwed up my life so I guess they didn't do a good job protecting me.

Something was going on in the vision. I took a deep breath and swam toward it.

"Epistofi stin patrida," Jocasta cast the spell on the water. "I found the boy. The lake is a portal that will take you to his location. Go!"

Cadmus didn't waste a second. He lowered himself into the water and dove under, swimming deeper and deeper until he found himself surrounded by white.

The navy blue ninja appeared right in front of me. I screamed out, the scream muffled by the water, and then I swam toward the surface. I was just inches from breaking the surface when his hand grabbed my ankle and pulled me down. I kicked with my free foot but he manipulated his arms around my legs to keep them from connecting with him in any significant way.

I screamed again, using the last amount of air I had. My lungs burned with the need for oxygen. I fought to free my legs as the ninja pulled me deeper in the pool. The floor of the pool shimmered like a curtain in the wind.

A flash of light hit the ninja and his grip loosened. I wiggled out and swam to the surface, gasping for air when my face left the water. The sorcerer that pretended to be Grandpa Atlas stood on the side of the pool. His arms were stretched out in front of him.

"Trey, get out of the pool," the Sorcerer yelled. The ninja surfaced a few feet to my right. I swam for the wall; I could hear the ninja trying to catch up to me. I grabbed the wall with both hands and started to pull myself out. My adopted parents ran towards me. I was almost out of the pool when the hands grabbed my shoulders and threw me backwards into the water.

The ninja came toward me under water. I punched and kicked at him as much as I could. I swam backwards, hoping to get to the other wall. The middle of the pool started swirling in front of me. A waterspout was sucking the water down to the floor of the pool.

"That's a portal," the Sorcerer yelled. "Stay away from it, Trey. They're trying to get you to Atlantis." I shifted my momentum away from the tornado and collided with the ninja. He wrapped his arms around me, constricting my arms like a snake.

"Help!" I screamed, water rushing into my mouth. He pushed and I fought to surface again. Spitting out the water, "Help!"

"Do something," Mom yelled.

"Trey, you have to break free," the Sorcerer instructed as the ninja pulled me under again.

The woman's face was in the center of the vortex now. Her evil smile sent shivers up and down my spine. She waved her hand, signaling me to come into the whirlpool. The ninja wasn't giving me the option; he swam toward the portal, still wrapped tight around me. This guy was stronger than anyone I'd ever known.

The spiraling water lit up in flames and the ninja, startled, released enough pressure for me to fight out of his grip. I kicked him, not even knowing where I connected with his body, and swam for the wall. I surfaced just inches from the wall and gasped in a huge breath. My lungs ached for air and my nose burned from the water it inhaled. I needed to rest but there was no time. The ninja moved towards me again.

"Trey, get out of the pool," the Sorcerer yelled. "Hurry!" I climbed onto the wall and collapsed, my exposed back lying on the cold concrete. The sorcerer raised his arms and swiped them apart. "Pagono!"

The sound of glass sliding on glass filled the air. I sat up and watched as the pool turned to solid ice with the ninja trapped inside. I breathed a sigh of relief and relaxed. Only a few seconds later, the sound of shattering ice echoed in the room. The block of ice had cracked in millions of pieces. Less than a second later, the ice melted and the pool was full of water again.

I looked for the ninja but instead I saw the woman from the vision, the one with the evil smile, climbing out of the pool on the opposite side.

"You have to go now," the Sorcerer said, looking at Mom, Dad, and me. "She's a very powerful sorceress. This is going to get ugly."

Mom pulled me to my feet and pushed me in front of her. Dad followed behind her. We made it to the door to leave the pool area but, as I pulled the door open, it was forced shut and the handle turned red-hot. I jerked my hand away and turned to look back at the pool.

"What are you doing here, Jocasta?" the Sorcerer asked the woman.

"I am ensuring the prophecy does not come true," she answered. "At least not in the way you want." She ran toward me, extended her hand, and began to shout "Paral...". She was knocked backwards as the Sorcerer shot his hands forward. Just that fast she was back on her feet and swiped her arms low at the ground. The move knocked the Sorcerer to the floor. Jocasta bent over him and smirked. "Paralyo". The Sorcerer went rigid, like a statue.

Jocasta turned her attention to the three of us standing by the exit. She walked slowly towards us. My Mom and Dad stepped in front of me. The Sorceress laughed with an evil hiss. "Fools. You are no match for me. Give me the boy and I won't harm you." My parents didn't even flinch.

Jocasta's voice filled with fury. "He is not even your son!" She whipped her hands in front of her and then pulled them apart. The move threw my parents to the bleachers, their bodies crashing and then laying as still as the Sorcerer.

"Mom!" I screamed. "Dad!" Suddenly the fact that I recently found out they were my adopted parents didn't matter anymore. I ran for the bleachers. Water shot out to the floor in front of me, I slid and crashed on my back, my head bouncing off the concrete. The room spun around me.

"It's just me and you now, boy" Jocasta bent over me. "Time for you to go home." I saw the ninja lean over next to her. He pulled me up and threw me into the pool. I sank, my head felt like

it had been split open. Seconds later, the ninja and Jocasta were

next to me.

The ninja pulled me to the surface and held me while Jocasta circled her hand in the water, creating a vortex again. "Epistofi stin patrida," she chanted and the image of the cavern reappeared, though it was fuzzy now that my head was throbbing.

Jocasta entered the portal first and I saw her disappear from the pool and reappear in the cave. The ninja pushed me towards the portal. I didn't have the strength to fight.

"Stamato!" the Sorcerer yelled from the wall. He lay on his stomach, his hand stretching toward us in the center of the pool. Locked in place, I couldn't physically move but I knew I wasn't paralyzed. "Kinoumai," he cast another spell, this time using his hand to move the ninja into the portal. The ninja was gone for a second and then he was in the cave next to Jocasta.

The whirlpool intensified and my body moved towards it without my control. Jocasta was swirling her hands in the cavern lake and the faster she circled, the more the velocity of the vortex increased.

"Help!" the scream sent throbbing pain through my head.

Mom was now next to the Sorcerer. "Do something," she cried.

"I can't stop it from pulling him in," he told her.

"They'll kill him if they get him," she pleaded.

"There is something I can do," he said. "It'll buy him a little time." The Sorcerer cut the air with his arm, "Chorizo! Epistofi stin patrida! Chorizo!"

The vortex pulled me in and I circled its edge for a few seconds, each time going deeper into the pool, until I was at the boundary of the portal. The world went black before I entered the floor.

"Where's the boy," Cadmus asked. "Shouldn't he have ended up here?"

Jocasta's face turned to fury. "The portal was split. The boy was sent somewhere else."

"Now what?"

An evil smile formed on the sorceress' face. "We wait."

Pain throbbed in my arms, back, and legs. I could feel the bruise on the back of my head. I tried to move but sharp pain shot through my head and I stopped and laid still. I ground my teeth and closed my eyes to fight the pain, trying to chase it from my mind.

Not relying on sight, I let my other senses interpret the world around me. A comfortable, soothing breeze swept around me. Plants rustled in the air that smelled clean and fresh. Drops of rain landed on my face and body. I wasn't in a cave. I opened my eyes and, as the image cleared up, I saw that I was in a forest. Green and dripping with rain, it reminded me of pictures of a rain forest. My necklace lit up and grew brighter from the drops of water that landed on it.

Lucky to be alive and awake, I tried to move again, this time with a little more success. I moved my legs to keep them from growing stiff. The pain a little more bearable than before. I was thankful that, probably because of the Sorcerer, I ended up here instead of in the cave with Jocasta and the ninja.

I heard the voices before I saw their sources but I didn't move to look. I didn't want to jeopardize my safety, the little that I had. If it was the ninja and Jocasta I was in trouble.

"Ekeinos n archi o foteinos," a young, male voice said.

I shocked myself when I understood that to mean, "there's the source of the light." How did I know how to speak Atlantean? How did I even know it was Atlantean?

"Esy orthos eisai," a woman said.

"Foteinos o einai proelefsi apo o basilikos kleidi," a man's voice said. "Mythos o einai alithinos."

"Ekeinos prepei noima aftos einai...," the woman stopped with a gasp.

The boy finished for the woman, "...mas basilias."

Protos Entyposi

They'd just had a conversation in Atlantean and, even though I shouldn't have understood any of it, I actually knew exactly what they'd said. They had said "the light was coming from the royal key and that means the legend is true." And then the woman said "that must mean he's…" and the boy finished "our Prince". This skill, though mysterious, would definitely come in handy.

The boy's hand stretched out to help me up. I took his hand in mine and he pulled me to my feet. The minute amount of pain that remained did not prevent me from standing or walking.

I stared at the boy, now standing in between a man and woman. The boy appeared to be a couple years younger than me. He had layered hair that looked a lot like mine, except it was dirty blond instead of pure blond. He had a smooth and handsome face. His eyes were blue, but not ocean like. He smiled at me and I smiled back.

"My name is Oaren," the boy said in Atlantean.

My first chance to find out if my mysterious, previously hidden, talent worked in reverse. Could I translate what I wanted to say and speak Atlantean? I wanted to tell him "I'm Trey." I concentrated hard and felt the words leave my mouth. "Onoma mou einai Trey."

It worked. It came out as "my name is Trey" but at least I could communicate. I grew up in Miami so I didn't learn the Atlantean language. I guess it was somehow built into me, like an instinct.

The adults standing next to the boy looked at me with a mixture of awe and concern. The woman had a tarnished face. I knew I would never guess her true age because she looked years older than her time. Her dark brown hair flowed to the middle of her back. The man had blond hair cut short and his eyes were the same blue as the boy's. In fact, I could see that the boy had the same facial features as the man. They were related, probably father and son.

Their clothes were also new to me. The woman wore a full-length tunic that looked very similar to a modern dress. The white fabric had a slight tint of brown from dirt. The man and the boy both wore tunics that matched the woman's but theirs covered only their waists to just above the knees. Their upper bodies, exposed, showed off large sea turtle tattoos on their upper arms. I couldn't tell if the woman had the tattoo because the dress covered her upper arm. They all wore leather-braided necklaces, like mine, but it looked like they had oyster pearls on them. And all three of them had leather sandals on.

The woman bowed, "My name is Kristjana." My mind automatically converted Atlantean to English.

The man bowed, "My name is Deon."

The woman continued. "Can I ask you how you got here, your Highness?"

I looked at her with a mixture of shock and confusion. Grandpa...the Sorcerer... was right; they did recognize me as a royal. I played dumb because I didn't know if I could trust these people just yet. I sent English words to my mouth but they came out in Atlantean. "I'm sorry?"

"You are our new prince," Oaren answered.

"Can someone explain what is going on?" I said. They stared at me, probably still in shock that they were standing in my presence. I knew how the ancient peoples worshiped their leaders. I had a feeling that the Atlanteans had many ancient people qualities, as evident by their dress and bowing.

I needed some more clarification. "I need you to start at the beginning, when you first saw me."

"Mom, Dad, and I saw light beaming up through the trees of the forest," Oaren began. So, as suspected, they were a family. "My dad recognized the light and said that it was produced by the royal key."

"The royal key is a legend told to every Atlantean," Deon said. "It was said that the key was cut by the sorcerer Aruc under the rule of

King Atlas thousands of years ago."

The light was seen and is recognizable. I hoped the ninjas and Jocasta didn't notice.

"So then you understand why we would refer to you as our prince?" Kristjana said.

"No, to be quite honest, I don't."

"Why don't you come back to our house?" Oaren suggested. "Mom can make you something to eat and drink. And we can explain what is happening and figure out why you are here."

"I already know why I'm here," I told him. I stopped myself and thought about what and how much I should tell them. I wasn't sure I wanted to tell them that I was actually born in Atlantis yet so I told them part of the story. "I decided to come here after I had visions of a woman in trouble."

"A woman in trouble?" Oaren sounded shocked. "Who?"

"Aerian," I answered. "She kept calling me...."

"Aerian?" Kristjana cut me off. "Forgive me, my Prince, but I am wondering how you know Aerian."

"She appeared to me in a vision and called on me for help. She told me to see the key. I'm not sure where she is but I know I have to help her."

"Well come back for something to eat and drink," Kristjana insisted. "After all, it's not every day I can serve the Prince of Atlantis."

"And maybe we can help you figure out how to find Aerian," Deon chimed in.

"Alright," I nodded. I had a million questions racing through my mind anyway and I figured it would be better to ask them while we sat around instead of in the middle of the woods.

"Where are you from?" Oaren asked as we began trekking through the woods. The rain had let up, but it wasn't easy to walk through the forest in a wet swimsuit. Small bushes and ferns covered the ground. Large deciduous trees towered into the sky. Vines hung from tree to tree. The air was warm but not as humid as I expected a rain forest to be..

Again, I decided to avoid telling them I was born in Atlantis. "I'm from Miami, Florida," I answered. "That's part of the United States. The United States is a country outside, to the, um..."

"We know the United States," Oaren replied. His "United States" came out perfectly clear. And then he did something I didn't expect. He spoke English, "So you speak English then?"

"Yeah," I said in English. "How do you know how to speak English?"

"We may be hidden from the world," Deon said. He too spoke English. "But the world is not hidden from us. Many of our people leave to explore other places and then come back and fill us in."

"We have to take English in school," Oaren informed me. "They say that many people know how to speak English so it can be a common language to unite us when we leave the island barrier. Many other languages are offered as well. We also take classes on the geography, culture, and history of the world."

"Which would explain the skyscrapers I saw in my visions," I said.

"Our city and culture, for better or worse, have been influen-ced by the outside world," Kristjana responded. "But we try to maintain some of our history. Which is why most of us still dress this way."

There was a pause before Oaren spoke, "But now the quest-ion is, how do you know how to speak Atlantean?"

"I don't know." I had an inclination that it had to do with the fact that I was an Atlantean but I didn't know that was the true reason and, even if it was, I didn't want them to know that. "I never learned it. In fact, two days ago, I didn't even know Atlantis existed."

"Atlantean uses many Greek words," Kristjana explained. "But our grammar, pronunciation, and use can be quite different. Did you ever learn Greek?"

"No," I said. "I don't know how I know."

We walked a few minutes without saying anything. The forest grew darker as night set in. "So where are we going?" I questioned.

"We are in the boreiodytikos dasos," Deon told me. "The northwest forest. We live on a farm on the edge of the forest. We'll be there soon."

He was right, in less than ten minutes, we stepped out of the forest into open farmland. The small amount of light left allowed me to see houses scattered around what seemed like one big field. A house sat straight ahead.

"That's ours," Oaren said, sounding proud as he pointed to the house I'd just noticed.

Behind that, I could see lots of lights in the far distance.

"And those lights are from the city," Oaren added.

"Good to see that even though you maintain your culture, you picked up the idea of electricity from the rest of the world," I said smiling.

"We did," Deon said, "but it's hydroelectricity."

"And not everyone embraces it," Kristjana added.

"Looks like I have a lot to learn about this place," I said as we approached the house.

"You are the ruling Prince," Kristjana said. "You will be surrounded by people to help you."

"So who is King?" I questioned.

"Well a male ruler is called the basilias and female ruler is basilissa," Kristjana explained. "We don't refer to our rulers as kings and queens because of all the damage done by those rulers in the past, like King Atlas and the ones that followed immediately after him.

"But the fourth ruler after King Atlas was Prince Soterios. And

Soterios insisted that people call him Prince because he did not want to be thought of in the same light as the previous rulers. It is said that he was one of the best rulers in Atlantean history. Ever since, our rulers have been princes and princesses, at least in English."

Deon opened the door and led us into the house. The kitchen looked old due to the rock walls but it had modern appliances and furniture. It appeared that all of their appliances ran on electricity. I wanted to find out more about the way their hydroelectric power worked to run the whole island.

"Oaren, why don't you show our Prince the rest of the house," Kristjana said. "I will fix us something to eat."

"Please, call me Trey," I told them. "You don't have to refer to me as Prince all the time".

"Forgive us if we do," Kristjana replied.

I nodded to show her I would accept that.

"Come on," Oaren said. He led me out of the kitchen. The next room had a table and chairs set. It had a large, ancient, dark wood hutch. Following Oaren through that room, I found myself standing in the equivalent of a living room. They had chairs, but not large comfortable ones like I was used to seeing. These were made of wood and only had a thin pad to sit on. They had a glass table that doubled as an aquarium with the most beautiful fish I had ever seen. The wall to the left had a large panel of water.

"What's that?" I asked Oaren and pointed to the panel of water.

"Watch," he said. He placed his hand on the panel and it lit up. Moments later, it was functioning like a television.

"That's cool."

"It looks cool but it really is not anything special, unless you like to keep up with what is going on. It is not like the ones I heard you have, where you can watch fake visions for entertainment."

I smiled. Fake visions? Obviously he'd never heard about reality TV. Come on, it doesn't get any better than that.

"There are bedrooms upstairs. My room and my parents' rooms are there. There is an extra one that you can use while you stay here. But I imagine it would only be tonight. You have an island to run."

"I think you're right," I told him. "I can't stay long because I have to find Aerian."

"Oh yeah, I almost forgot. We can work on that tomorrow though. Let's get something to eat and a good night's sleep."

By the time I finished touring the house, ate a very delicious salmon and fresh vegetables dinner, and told the family all about my life at home, I was ready for bed. Oaren showed me to the spare room and made sure everything was satisfactory.

My mind raced. I lay in bed, tired but unable to sleep. I had a great first impression of the island but I was overwhelmed. There were people that wanted me dead and they now knew I existed. I'd been attacked for the first time in my life and now I was on a foreign island.

I was alone and unprotected. I didn't even have my parents, adopted parents, to tell me that everything was alright.

But my biological parents were somewhere on the island. *Hopefully.* So I needed to find out as much about the island and use it to my advantage. And the part that concerned me the most was that I didn't just have to learn the history, geography, and culture for my own goals; these people wanted me to use that knowledge to take charge of Atlantis.

Aftokinero

I opened my eyes and felt lost for a moment. I didn't recog-nize the room around me. I racked the back of my brain to try to figure out where I was and how I got there. As sleep slowly crept out, my memory of yesterday came back to me. I was in a house, in Atlantis. It was real and now my true mission was about to begin.

I sat up and swung my legs off the low-lying bed. The wooden bed frame had a very thin, quite uncomfortable mattress. I guess I was lucky I was so tired or I might not have slept well. Stretching, I went to the window and looked outside.

A mixture of orange, red, purple, blue, and a slight tinge of green filled the morning sky. Low lying clouds that looked like streams of water running through the sky seemed to stretch on, and interconnect, for quite a distance. I stared at them for a few minutes.

If only I had real clothes, instead of just the swimsuit to wear. I'd thought Oaren could loan me some clothes but he didn't offer.

Somehow though, I had to get new clothes. I decided to head downstairs and see if anyone was up.

When I got to the bottom of the steps, I could hear Kristjana, Deon, and Oaren talking in the kitchen. They spoke in Atlantean again but, like yesterday, I could understand it.

"He seems nice," I heard Oaren. "I think he is going to make a great Prince."

"With help and some training," Deon said, "I agree."

Kristjana chimed in. "There is something special about that boy. I don't know what it is yet but I can see it in his eyes. I can feel it when he is around us. He is not normal."

Not normal? My gut twisted and my heart dropped. It was like she was stabbing me in the back. First I find out that the people at home were not who I thought they were and then the first Atlanteans I met thought I wasn't normal. Would I fit in anywhere?

"He does have something about him that is just..." Deon added, "special."

"Maybe it is a good sign," Oaren said.

"Oh it is definitely good," Kristjana told him. "I didn't mean it was a bad thing. No. I think it is going to be a great thing. He has something in his eyes I have never seen before. I just don't know what it means."

That was better. So I wasn't normal, but in a good way. I could live with that.

"But someone needs to help him find Aerian," Deon said. "He's going to need someone that knows the ins and outs of the island. Because at this point, he doesn't know anything about navigating this island."

"Well I want to take him into the city today," Kristjana said. "I want him to get to the tailors and get a tunic so that he looks like an Atlantean Prince. The tailor will surely give him the tunic for royals once she sees him."

"I'm going with," Oaren said.

"I need your help on the farm," Deon told him.

"But I want to guide him. Why can't I be the one to lead him around the island in his quests? Think about how great it would be for your son to be an adviser to the ruling Prince."

Basilias, that's what I was. They had said that it meant 'prince'.

"I think that would be wonderful," Kristjana supported Oaren. "Why shouldn't it be you? You definitely know your way around the island. You would be perfect for answering his questions about geography and the culture."

"And what about the help I need?" Deon said.

"I can help," Kristjana said. "And we can get someone to help if we need too."

"You're going to help me today?" Deon asked.

There was silence for a moment. I decided to go into the kitchen.

"Good morning," they all greeted me, in English, with a bow. They were dressed like they were yesterday, though not the same clothes. Oaren and Deon had tunics that were not dirty, just pure white. Deon wore a top that had a 'V' shape cutout over his chest. Oaren's tunic covered his waist to his knees. I noticed the tattoo on his arm again. Kristjana's dress was white and sleeveless. She didn't have a tattoo on her arm. I had questions about the tattoos, but I figured I would wait until Oaren and I had a chance to talk and I would just ask him.

"You don't have to bow to me," I told them. They didn't respond to that.

"How did you sleep?" Kristjana asked.

"Good, thanks," I answered.

"Do you need anything?" she questioned. "Something to eat or drink?"

"Some water would be great," I said. "And I'd really like to wash up and get some new clothes.

Oaren went to the cupboard, got a cup, filled it with water, and then handed it to me.

"You can wash off in the river," Kristjana told me. "Oaren is going to take you into the city so you can get some clothes."

I took a sip of water. "That's great!"

Deon watched me carefully. "Oaren, make sure you take him to the royal guard office while you are in the city."

"No!" Kristjana cut in. "The royal guard has been infiltrated by the Knights of the Abyss. If you take him into their office, they will know he is here and they will kill him."

"I figured they could help him get the materials he needs," Deon explained himself. "And I thought they could help him find Aerian."

"I can take him into the palace and see if we can gather some materials," Oaren suggested.

"The palace is definitely in the control of those blue ninja guys."

"The Knights of the Abyss," Kristjana said.

"Yeah, the Knights of the Abyss," I continued. "They have control of the palace. If we go to the palace, I'm doomed."

"If they are in control of the palace," Oaren said, "why are they not killing civilians and changing laws?"

"The Knights of the Abyss are not interested in harming Atlantean civilians," Kristjana said. "They are only interested in killing royalty. I imagine that in a few days, they will in fact start putting laws into place and trying to control everyday life. But that's going to take time."

"I don't understand why the Atlantean military didn't fight back against the Knights," I said.

"The Knights of the Abyss were hidden amongst the soldiers and royal guards," Kristjana said. "Once the Knights gained control of the palace, they had the advantage of being inside the royal grounds, which provides a great defensive advantage. Also, without a royal to make decisions, the military wouldn't have been very organized."

"So what do you want me to do?" Oaren asked to get us back on track with the original discussion..

"Take him to the city and get him clothes. Stop by the

Geografikos and get him a map of the island. When the two of you make it back tonight, we will look into how to find Aerian. Just make sure the Knights don't recognize him as the Prince."

I knew that was going to be harder than they expected since Jocasta and that Knight already knew about me. Oaren nodded to show he understood what she said. I finished my water and then

headed to the river to freshen up from the attack and wet forest

trek.

After I washed off, I met Oaren outside the house. Not a single cloud in the blue sky, except those long, strange streams in the air. The air was warm with sunlight as it hit my skin. A few skyscrapers in the distance gave me a hint of the city.

"This is going to be a long walk isn't it?" I said. "Maybe we should forget the new clothes and look for Aerian."

Oaren ignored me and instead, as Deon walked by, said, "Mporo ego pairno o aftokinero?"

My jaw dropped and I looked at him, trying to figure out if I'd heard him correctly.

"Oche," Deon responded sternly.

"Egol zito Mana," Oaren defied.

"Oche," Deon said again.

Kristjana walked past on her way to the field, carrying milking buckets for the cows.

"Mana," Oaren went ahead with asking her, "mporo ego pairno o aftokinero?"

"Oche," Deon answered before Kristjana had a chance.

"You should let him," said Kristjana. Deon pulled her to the side and began discussing something with her.

"Did you really ask that?" I looked at Oaren. He smiled and I could tell that I was correct in my interpretations. "Are you old enough?"

"No age limit to drive them," he answered.

"Can you take the aftokinero?" I said. "The Water Car?"

"Exactly," he said. He pointed up to the long clouds in the sky. "Those clouds are streams of water. The aftokineros actually float, like boats, but the water propels them. The front of the car sucks up the water, it passes through many tubes and shoots out the back of the car, thereby propelling them. And it only needs electricity when you start it up, to get the first amount of water in. After that the water movement powers it.

"You've got to be kidding me," I laughed with the biggest smile ever. "That's awesome! Roads in the sky."

He smiled when he saw the look on my face. "And the water provides the energy, which is stored, for the next time the car is started. They are really fun to drive too. But Dad never lets me take it out. It's so much faster to take the aftokinero though. Walking could take us hours, where as with the aftokinero it would be minutes."

"You can take it," Deon said after he finished discussing it with Kristjana. He turned and headed down the field.

"Be careful," Kristjana said. "And come back before dark."

"Yes, Mom," Oaren jumped victoriously and ran opposite the way Deon had just walked. I followed him, running fast to catch up, then jogging aside of him.

"She acts like I never went to the city by myself before."

"What will she do if we're not back by dark?" I asked.

"It is not Mom we have to worry about if we are in the city after dark," Oaren replied.

I looked at him, confused. He must have noticed that I wanted further explanation.

"Let's just say the city is not nice after dark. There are a lot of criminal activities that take place."

"Like any other city I can think of," I said.

"You are probably thinking that Atlantis is this beautiful, per-fect island civilization. The truth is, there are very dark things that take place here. We have not even scratched the surface with what we told you. The city can be a very dangerous place. It is much different than living on the farm."

We got to the river and I saw the aftokinero sitting against the

bank, tied to a tree. It was made of a silver, metal-looking substance. "Isn't that too heavy to sit on those streams in the air? Won't it fall through?"

"It is made of hydrome," said Oaren. "It is a metal found only here in Atlantis. The same metal that is in your necklace; very strong but also very light." Oaren jumped into the aftokinero and sat in the driver's seat, which was black and very padded. The wheel in front of him looked like a boat steering wheel.

"Come on," he said. "Get in."

I hopped in and sat down in the seat next to him.

"Take the rope off the hook right there," he instructed.

I disconnected the rope from the peg on the door and we were free from the tree.

There was a clear substance on the front, where the windshield is on a normal car. "Is that glass?"

"Yes, reinforced glass. We put some of our minerals in it and it makes it sturdy." Oaren dipped his left hand in the water and rubbed it on the steering wheel. The car seemed to wake up from a deep sleep.

"Poios einai odigisi?" asked a voice from the car.

Oaren told it he was the one driving. I heard a zap of electricity within the car and it started sucking water in, very quietly. I thought I would feel the water running through the car but I didn't.

"Hang on," Oaren said. He pulled down on a lever next to the wheel and the aftokinero roared as it sucked a wave of water in and pushed it out with a force I've never experienced. "Every force has an equal and opposite force," he smiled at me.

The car shot straight up into the air as the water shot out from underneath. The force pushed us right into a water stream in the air and Oaren quickly moved the lever to the middle position. And with that, we raced down a stream in the air.

"We call these streams of water 'synnero'," Oaren told me. "That means 'water cloud'"

"How do they keep the synnero in the air?"

"Static electricity," he told me. "The scientists put a few slight charges through the air, where they want the synnero, and the water is forced to stay in place. The charges are constantly being sent out from a source in the city. You do not notice them though."

"Static electricity? With water?"

"Water's oxygen atom is slightly negative and its hydrogen atoms are slightly positive. The scientists use that to their advantage. I do not know where the static electrical charges go but that's how it works."

I remembered doing an experiment with my mom as a kid. We rubbed a comb through our hair and then put it up to a stream of water running out of the sink faucet. We could move the stream by moving the comb near the stream of water. That was the same concept. "I get it," I told him. I didn't want him to think I was a complete idiot. Apparently, like most countries, Atlantis was far ahead of us in science.

I sat back and took in the site of the fields below us. Other aftokineros raced down the synneros around us. The wind whipped at me; it felt great. It was like doing a hundred miles an hour down a highway in a convertible with the top down.

"Let's go faster," Oaren yelled over the wind. He pulled the lever down and the aftokinero gained velocity.

"WOOOHOOO!" I yelled.

"Now you are living," Oaren said.

My stomach wrenched as Oaren turned the wheel to the right and connected with a different synnero. He must've noticed my face because he laughed. "You will get used to it."

The city grew larger and clearer as we approached. I could see

four skyscrapers and lots of smaller buildings. Some of the smaller buildings looked similar to the buildings found in Miami but a lot of them had the look of ancient Greek and Egyptian architecture. A large sand colored wall stood on the outside of the city. Anticipation ate at me as I studied the city. I had always been fascinated with the idea of city walls protecting the buildings and people inside them.

"We are approaching drop point," Oaren told me as we flew over the wall. He slowed the aftokinero down to a near stop. "This is going to get your stomach good." He pushed the lever all the way up to where it was when we got in the aftokinero. Just that fast, we fell out of the sky, straight down and landed in a river.

Basilikos Roucha kai ena Ektakto Geografikos

Oaren tied the aftokinero to the dock as I scoped out the city around me. Four skyscrapers towered over the other buildings. Some of the buildings were large, marble structures that were distinctly ancient Greek architecture. Some resembled modern businesses with glass front windows. There were even some that were made of marble and had some Greek architecture mixed with modern qualities.

People bustled from business to business on the streets. I definitely stood out in my swimsuit as everyone I could see wore tunics of varying lengths and colors. Many people stopped and stared at me. I watched to see if anyone showed any signs of knowing that I was royalty. I didn't want to be picked out as the Prince. Not when anyone could be an enemy that was looking to kill royals.

Oaren stepped aside of me. "Welcome to the city of Atlantis," he said. "This will really give you an idea of the culture."

"I'm not here for a tour," I told him. "There will be a time for that. We need to quickly, and quietly without being seen by too many people, get some clothes and a map of the island. Then we need to get home and find Aerian. The longer we stay here, the more chance I have of being noticed as a royal."

"Trey, you are already noticed," Oaren told me. "These people know who you are."

I watched the people. They were all going about their business but they all had one thing in common. They stared at me as they carried on with their activities. "But they're not bowing," I said.

"They do not want you to be picked out by the Knights," he said. "The Knights are going to know soon enough, especially if one spots you. They do not want to speed that process up."

"So the Atlanteans definitely do not like the Knights of the Abyss?"

"In general, definitely not. Most Atlanteans, though not all, were happy with the royal family. In fact, I'm sure if the Knights put any kind of laws or pressure on the civilians, there will be an uprising."

"Well we don't want that to start today," I said. "I'm not ready yet. Let's go get some clothes."

He led me down the pavement. People either gawked or smiled brightly at me. I loved the attention but I needed to have a conversation with Oaren so it was awkward. "It's warm today," I said randomly.

"This is the normal temperature," he said. "The barrier keeps us pretty insulated. We have our own weather patterns and storms. Even our weather is not influenced by the outside world."

"Do you get a lot of rain?" I asked.

"Just the showers that you..." He pushed me in the alley between two buildings. "Stop!"

"What?!"

"There were Knights of the Abyss walking towards us." He stared out of the alley for a moment. "You stay here. If they see you, we are in trouble." He walked out of the alley and turned right, to go the same direction we were just walking. I backed up and rested against the wall of the building.

Oaren reentered the alley. "The clothing place is four shops

up. The Knights turned off and are now walking a different direction. We can go but we should hurry." We left the alley and walked briskly up four shops to a building made of marble with large glass windows in front. Six marble steps led up to the entrance. One pillar sat on each side of the door. A large sign that read "Moda Raftis" hung above the door.

"Trendy Tailor," I said in English.

"Inside," Oaren ignored me, "quick!" I walked up the steps and went into the shop. Oaren followed behind me, keeping an eye on the window.

A large woman walked out of a back room and toward us.

"Kalosorizo," she said, "pos mporo ego boitho esy?" She had brown hair and was wearing a white dress that reminded me of a bed sheet.

"He speaks English," Oaren told her.

"Oh my," the woman gasped. "You are... oh my." She bowed to me.

"We don't have much time," I told her. "I need tunics and I need to get them quick before the Knights find me."

"Of course, my Prince," she said. "I have the best tunics in Atlantis. The royal family always ordered from me." Her facial expression changed from a hopeful surprise to one of sadness. "I knew almost the entire family. Such a shame, they were all such beautiful people. I can not believe they even murdered the kids."

"Can we just get the tunics?" Oaren said, his voice filled with impatience.

"Right away," she hurried away before she finished the statement.

I looked around the shop while she looked for tunics for me in the back. Most of the clothes in the front of the store were white and dull looking. There were leather sandals, like the ones Oaren wore, on the shelves against the wall. I walked over and looked at them.

"Those are not the ones you get," Oaren laughed as he joined me at the wall.

I looked at him with confusion. "What do you mean?"

"You are a Prince; you get the best clothes on the island."

"But I don't want to dress like a Prince since I don't want to be noticed."

He laughed again. "How many times did I tell you? Everyone can already tell you are a royal. You look just like one. And that necklace, if they see it, makes it a solid assumption. So, if they can already tell you are a Prince, then why not dress like one and show them you are proud of it. Show us that you are ready to lead us. Make a statement and tell us, I will lead your revolution to take back this island."

"Is that what these people want? I'm just here to find Aerian." I knew better but I still wanted to play dumb. I trusted Oaren more and more every minute but I still couldn't be absolutely sure he wasn't going to sell me out so I pretended that I didn't know everything I knew.

The woman joined us before Oaren could respond. "I have a number of tunics that will fit you," she said. "These were being prepared for Prince Jedrick..." She took a breath. "He was built like you. Try one on, you will want to wear it out of here anyway, and you can just take the rest of them."

"How much do they cost?" I asked. I didn't have any money, let alone Atlantean money.

The woman chuckled. "The Prince does not pay for his clothes." She handed me a seaweed green tunic bottom and a top, as well as a pair of boxers. I was relieved to find out that Atlanteans took to our boxers. At least some piece of clothing would be familiar.

"Now wait," she said before bustling to the back again. A minute later she returned with brown leather boots. "These are

royal shoes. They protect your feet more than sandals."

"Well, go put it on," Oaren was watching the window again.

"You can use the room back there to change," the woman told

me.

I walked to the back room and put the clothes and boots down on a table. It was a storage room and it didn't have a door. I couldn't get privacy by shutting a door so I stepped to the side where I didn't think Oaren and the woman would be able to see me. I wanted to get changed as quickly as possible so I undressed, slid the boxers on, and then wrapped the lower part of the tunic around my waist.

I sat it as low on my waist as possible so that it would reach down to my knees. I pulled the tunic tight against my waist, wrapped it, and made sure it wouldn't fall down. When I was sure it was tightly in place, I picked up the top and slipped it over my head. It was sleeveless and cut in a 'V' shape at the neck. I pulled on it to get it to stretch and meet the cloth already at my waist but it wouldn't reach all the way down. The V cut was too large and the necklace sat against my skin, exposed. I wouldn't be able to hide the necklace anymore.

I slipped the boots on, which were actually quite comfortable,

and headed out to the main area of the store. "I'm not sure it fits," I said. "The top doesn't meet the bottom."

Oaren and the woman both laughed like I told the funniest joke ever. I felt my face flush with embarrassment. Here I was, standing in a skirt and a top that didn't even cover my stomach and they were laughing at me. I was used to wearing jeans that fit snuggly and t-shirts that were large enough to go past my waist. Although the fabric was comfortable, my opinion of what was appropriate to wear made me feel uncomfortable.

"They are not supposed to meet," the woman explained. "Believe it or not, that actually fits perfectly." They were still laughing.

"It's not funny," I told them. " This is the stuff the girls I go out with wear. This looks good on a girl, not a guy."

The woman stopped laughing. "Actually it looks great on you. Wait until the Atlantean girls see you, you won't be able to keep them away."

"She is right," Oaren said. "The girls here are used to guys in tunics. They are not going to find jeans and t-shirts attractive. And royal tunics are even better than the ones I buy. The royal ones are custom fit and so they conform to your body. Mine do not do that."

"And because you and Jedrick were the same size," the woman continued, "these conform to your body the way you want."

I felt even more embarrassed. A woman older than my mom and a guy younger than me, talked about how the tunic conformed to my body. I didn't even know what to say to get them to stop making me feel worse.

The woman composed herself. "I will get you a bag." She took the other tunics to the back. When she came back, she carried a large cloth bag. "Jedrick had ordered four outfits and two pairs of boots, so the others are in the bag. I will start working on more for you." She looked at me with satisfaction.

"Thanks," I said, even though I wasn't thankful that this was going to be my new style of clothing.

"One last thing," the woman said as she scurried to the left side of the shop. "You need a belt to hold a sword and other things." She handed me a black rope.

I immediately tied it around my waist so that my bottom piece was even more likely to stay on. "Thanks."

"That's everything," she said.

"Alright." I smiled uncomfortably.

"Are you going to battle the Knights of the Abyss?" she asked.

"I'm going to find the girl I am looking for," I answered.

"There's always a girl involved for good looking boys like you," she replied.

I ignored her and continued, "After that, I don't know what's going to happen."

"I hope you take back the island. The royal family deserves vengeance."

"We should get going," I said, looking at Oaren.

"Definitely," he agreed.

"Be careful, my Prince," the woman showed concern in her face.

Oaren and I left the shop and immediately searched for signs of the Knights of the Abyss. Aftokineros moved above the city buildings. "I think the map place is to the left," Oaren said. "About ten shops down. We need to go quickly and carefully."

As we walked, I pulled on my top again, trying to get it to reach my waist but was unsuccessful.

"That is why I usually do not wear a top," Oaren told me. "It is more comfortable to go without one. Plus it helps attract the girls."

The Atlanteans had some strange ways of saying things. 'It helps attract the girls' was not the way I would phrase it. It sounded too formal. In fact, their entire use of the English language sounded too formal. After all, they rarely used contractions when speaking in English.

"Do you have a girlfriend?" I asked Oaren.

"No. There is a someone at school that I really like though."

"When do you go to school?"

"I am on break at the moment."

"How old are you?"

"Fourteen, almost fifteen, years old." He looked at me. "How about you?"

"I'm sixteen. I'm missing school at the moment. And I don't have one steady girlfriend but I date lots of girls." I noticed the people around us were staring at me again.

I saw someone that looked like a soldier staring at me intently. He had silver armor over his black tunic and a sword at his side. "Is he a soldier?" I asked Oaren.

He studied the guy for a minute. "Yes. See the tattoo on his arm? It is a medousa...sorry, jellyfish."

"I can speak Atlantean," I reminded him. "I don't know how I can, but I can."

"The medousa tattoo is the symbol of the military."

I thought about that for a moment. I remembered that Oaren had a sea turtle tattoo on his arm. "Does your tattoo have a meaning?"

"All of the tattoos have meanings. It tells you what class that person is in. People with sea turtles, like myself, are the laborers. We are the farmers, tailors, factory workers and so on. Soldiers have jellyfish tattoos. The upper class, people that are considered elites, have starfish tattoos. And the royals have a seahorse, which you will need to get at some point."

No way was I getting a tattoo but I wasn't about to argue at this point. Besides, we were actually at the map shop. A modern looking building stood in front of us with a sign on the window that read, "Geografikos". Oaren opened the door for me and we walked in.

"He speaks English," Oaren started the conversation with the man that worked in the shop. "Yes, he is the new Prince. Yes, he knows that the Knights of the Abyss are killing the royals. What we need from you is a map of the island; the best you have would be great."

The man stood silent for a moment. Then he said, "I actually have one that just came in yesterday. It just so happens that a Knight brought it in. I think it came from the palace. The Knights were selling things all day yesterday."

"Can we see it?" Oaren asked. He was the one that would know if it was worth anything, since he knew what a map of Atlantis should look like.

The man went behind the marble topped counter and opened a drawer. He pulled out a piece of old parchment. "They sold it to me for very little. But this map would work well for you, my Prince. It is very valuable. They must not have realized it."

I looked at it. It looked like a normal, ancient map. "What is so special about it?" Oaren asked.

"First, it will show you any amount of detail you want," the man informed us. "From the whole island all the way to the layout of a specific building." I watched as the map zoomed in on the island until it showed the building we were in.

"That's like a really advanced GPS," I exclaimed. The man and Oaren didn't understand what I'd said and they didn't seem to care either.

"I have seen maps do that before," Oaren told him.

"Indeed you have," the man replied. "But that is not what makes this map so special. This one has a special curse on it."

"A curse?" I looked at him with concern.

"That does not mean it is bad," Oaren informed me. "It just means it is...," he thought for a moment, "...enchanted." He looked to see if I understood and then asked, "What curse?"

"Well, do you see all of the shops on this row?" the man questioned.

"Yes. So what?" Oaren didn't seem to care.

"Do you also notice that the shop across the street has four glowing red dots in it?" The man asked with a smile.

Oaren and I both looked closely at the map. The man was right. The shop across the street, which according to the map was a sword shop, was glowing with red dots.

"What does that mean?"

"It means that someone in that shop wants to do one of us harm," the man explained.

My heart started racing and my stomach twisted. By the looks of it, Oaren felt the same way I did. "Who?" Oaren asked.

We all looked out the window as four Knights of the Abyss, dressed in dark blue ninja outfits, walked out of the sword shop.

Anakalypto

The four Knights of the Abyss looked up and down the row of businesses. People walked by, ignoring them. It was obvious that the citizens didn't like the Knights.

"Back away from the window," Oaren told me. I backed up against the wall where they would be less likely to see me. Oaren went to the window and watched the Knights. The man went behind the counter and pretended to be busy studying a map but I could tell he was secretly watching the Knights. It wouldn't be good for him if they came in here and found me and he knew it.

I quickly walked to the counter and grabbed the special map. I watched, seeing glowing red on the space outside the sword shop. They weren't moving.

A moment later, Oaren shouted in panic, "Where can he hide? They are coming this way." The glowing red dots moved toward the map shop.

The man pointed to a cupboard sitting against the wall. I ran over and forced my way into the small wooden cupboard. It was a tight fit but it beat the alternative.

I could hear the four Knights enter the shop, speaking to each other in Atlantean. Oaren said, "Thank you" to the shop owner and—I guessed—left the shop.

"How can I help you?" asked the shop owner.

"The map that we gave you yesterday," a deep voice said, "we need it back."

I looked at the map in my hands. The red glow was very strong on the map shop.

"I'm sorry sir," the man said, "but I already sold it. You sold it to me cheap so I was able to sell it cheap and an old man interested in ancient maps bought it early this morning."

"Who?" asked the voice.

"I do not collect the names of my customers."

"Well now that the Knights of the Abyss are in control, you will. This will be a new procedure for all shops. We will want to know who is buying the items sold on a daily basis."

"Sir, I do believe that is something that should be discussed," the map owner countered.

"It was discussed," the Knight cut him off. "We discussed it and decided that we need to know if the civilians are planning a revolution."

"And how would that map help?"

"We discovered that it has a special...property," said a different voice.

"Well I am very sorry but it was already sold," the shop owner said.

"To the boy that was just in here?" asked the first voice.

"No. I already told you that I sold it to an old man interested in collecting ancient maps."

"I think you are lying."

"Now why would the boy want that map? And why would I lie to you?"

"Get that boy," the voice instructed the others. "I will stay here with this man. If the boy has the map, it will be most unfortunate for both of you. And if he does not—well—I am not making any promises."

I listened to the footsteps of the Knights leaving. I couldn't tell how many left but I was certain that the one with the deep voice stayed in the shop. "Let's just wait and see," he said.

I had to do something. I couldn't just sit here and wait for them to capture Oaren and bring him back. They would probably kill him and the shop owner. I had to come up with a plan.

I was fast from running every day. If I made it out of the cupboard, the shock of me bursting out would probably hinder the Knight, and I could run out of the shop and try to find Oaren. If I followed the red glow on the map, I would at least know where the Knights were. But if even one thing went wrong, that would be the end. And I wasn't sure if I would be able to get my normal speed in my new outfit and boots.

Here I was, stuffed in a cupboard to hide from a group of men that, if they knew I was here, would kill me because I was the new Prince. And Oaren was now somewhere in the city being hunted like an animal. It was clear the Atlanteans wanted a hero, someone who could lead them against the Knights and take back the island. Someone who was going to then lead them to prosperity. And they thought I was that person.

At some point, I was going to have to stop hiding and actually try to change things. I was going to have to fight to find and rescue Aerian. And I was going to have to fight to stay alive while we put a stop to the Knights of the Abyss. After all, Jocasta and one Knight knew I was alive and they probably figured out I was on the island by now. So, why not start now?

I hurled myself through the door of the cupboard and rolled across the floor. I scattered and climbed to my feet as quickly as possible. I saw the Knight turn to face me but didn't stop to watch what happened next. Just that fast I was out the door of the shop and running after the Knights, who I watched on the map I was holding.

Surprisingly, the tunic and boots didn't slow me down. In fact, I think they actually allowed me to run faster.

"Stop that boy," shouted the deep voice behind me. He followed me out of the store. I made my legs run even faster. I could see the three Knights up ahead and I was closing in fast. They had Oaren surrounded. This was it. This was the beginning of my adventure. There was no going back now. In a matter of minutes, they would discover that I had royal blood. And the word would spread to their entire group.

"Stop him," shouted the voice. No one bothered to try

but the three Knights a few shops ahead with Oaren heard the order. They turned to face me and two of them came towards me. Oaren remained hostage with a Knight holding a sword to his throat.

I had to act fast. Two came at me from the front and one followed behind me. I turned right, into an alley, and noticed that there was a brick wall in front of me. I had two options. Either climb the wall or be trapped. I scaled the wall in seconds, thanks to gym class, and hopped to the other side. I stopped to take a breather.

"Go around," ordered the deep voice. Then I heard him climbing the wall. He got to the top and I turned and stared at him. The navy cloth covered every piece of him except his dark eyes. They bore a hole through me.

He balanced himself on top of the wall. His eyes connected with the exposed pendant of my necklace and his eyes flickered like fire. I was discovered.

I decided to play mind games and show him that I wasn't afraid of him, even though I was terrified. It was just like when I was nervous about the swim meet but showed Ashley that I was confident and calm. My dad always said, "People won't judge you on what you are feeling or thinking inside, but on what you allow

them to see".

I showed the Knight the map and gave him the most confi-

dent smile I could. Then I rolled the map up and stuffed it in my belt. The fire in his eyes grew stronger and I knew it was time to run again.

The Knight jumped off the wall and, before he hit the ground, I was in a full sprint in the opposite direction. I got to the edge of the alley and turned right. I crashed over a box that was in front of a store and fell to the ground. I fought the pain to get to my feet and started running again, this time not as fast. The Knight was right behind me; he didn't fall over the box.

I picked up speed as my legs worked past the pain of the fall. As I approached another opportunity to turn into an alley, I also saw a chance to get ahead of the Knight. A wooden crate sat in front of a grocery store. I stopped, picked the crate up, and threw it at the Knight. He pushed it away, but in the mean time, I dove at his legs, and he fell over me.

I scrambled to my feet and started running back the way I just came. Lucky I did; when I looked back at the Knight I just took out, I saw the other two round the corner I was going to turn down.

I had to go back and get Oaren. So I backtracked the way I

just came and scaled the brick wall again. I went through the side door of the building that I knew Oaren and the Knight stood in front of. It was a pharmacy and I headed to a spot against the sidewall where I could see out the window. Sure enough, Oaren and the Knight were still standing there. The Knight no longer had his sword at Oaren's throat.

I pulled the map out of my belt and opened it. The red glow in front of the pharmacy indicated the Knight with Oaren. Another glowing red spot moved toward the pharmacy. Even more glowing red spots painted the buildings nearby. I knew, when I made the save, we would have to be quick because, in a matter of minutes, we would be surrounded. I rolled the map up again and returned it to my belt.

"Prince," a voice whispered in Atlantean. I turned to face a man with gray hair. He stood with a look of concern and a sword in his hand. "Here," he handed me the sword. "Take this. I saw you when you were at the map shop and I wanted to help. I own the sword shop and that is the best sword I have. It is for royalty only."

I studied the sword. It had a jagged, silver blade connected to a black handle that twisted to meet a seahorse at the end of it. It was light but I knew that the jagged edges would do a lot of damage to a body. "Thanks," I said, looking up. The man was gone.

I gripped the sword tightly and bolted out of the pharmacy. With an angry scream I never heard myself make before, I stabbed the Knight in the stomach. He collapsed to the ground, screaming and writhing in pain.

"Let's go," I told Oaren and started walking. He followed. "The Knights of the Abyss are all around us. I saw them on the map."

Three Knights, the ones that were chasing me, came around a corner in front of us. "Just great," Oaren said. We stopped walking, I gripped the sword as tightly as I could, and extended it in front of my body. I had just used a sword for the first time when I stabbed the Knight. Desperate times called for desperate measures.

The Knights approached and stopped a few feet in front of us, their swords drawn as well. "Anakalypto, Basilias," said the Knight with the deep voice.

"Why don't I know what 'anakalypto' means?" I asked Oaren.

"He said that you have been discovered, Prince," he told me.

I thought for a moment. I needed to show them again that I wasn't afraid of them. "I'm here to take my island back," I said with confidence.

The Knight with the deep voice charged at me and I prepared to block his sword with my own. My eyes closed instinctively, I heard the clang of metal on metal. I opened my eyes and found the soldier I saw earlier fighting off the three Knights. He held his own against the Knights so I just watched.

"GO!," the soldier turned to us as soon as he had a chance. Oaren and I didn't think twice; we ran away from the scene, swords clanging behind us.

"Where are we going now?" I asked.

"To the aftokinero," Oaren answered. "Time to get out of the city."

ADIKIA

Deon and Kristjana sat on the edge of their seats at the kitchen table as they listened to Oaren and I recap what happened in the city. It was obvious that, even though they expected the Knights to discover me, it was a thrilling story to hear. I, on the other hand, was not thrilled by it. In fact, I was now worried about the fact that the Knights definitely knew I was on the island. Up until now, I didn't know if Jocasta and the Knight knew I was on the island but now there was no doubt. What would they do to get to me? Would they come here and attack this family? And would they take their anger out on Aerian?

Kristjana prepared a traditional Atlantean salad, with lettuce, olives, tomatoes, peppers, and she had some chicken on top. Oaren explained most of what happened as I focused on eating my salad. I wanted to concentrate on finding Aerian, not on what happened earlier.

"So you got the clothes you needed, and the map," Kristjana recapped. "But then, when the Knights came looking for the map that they sold to the map shop, they found out that you exist and tried to kill you."

"And they would have," Oaren told her, "except for that sol-dier that saved us."

"But you don't know who he is?" Deon said.

"No," Oaren looked deep in thought.

"So this map glows red whenever someone is around that wants to cause harm to people near the map?" Kristjana probed for more.

"That's what the man at the map shop showed us," said Oaren.

"And it works," I added. "I was able to watch the Knights on the map and it allowed me to know where they were. It will be very useful when we start to look for Aerian." I hoped the hint would work.

"Any idea where she is?" asked Deon.

"No," Oaren and I answered at the same time.

"So how do you plan to find her?" Deon helped himself to more salad.

"I don't know," I replied. "That's the whole reason I haven't started looking for her. I wanted to search the city and hope that someone knew where she was but now I don't even want to be in the city. At least until I get some backup and supplies."

"But now that they know you exist, their one and only goal is going to be to hunt you down and kill you," Kristjana said with concern.

"I know that," I replied. In fact, they already did hunt me down. "But I have to help Aerian before they find me. If I can just gather up some soldiers and weapons."

"How did you connect with her before?" Kristjana asked.

"She seemed to appear to me when I was in water," I told her.

"Then maybe you should go swimming in the river," Oaren replied.

That wasn't a bad idea. I had thought about it a few times but was too focused on other things to actually do it. But now was as good a time as any. "Maybe I will," I said as I stood up. I made sure my tunic was still tight on my waist and pulled on the top, trying to stretch it again.

"Do yourself a favor and just take the shirt off," Oaren told me. "Especially if you are going to go swimming."

I looked at him. I didn't expect to go swimming in my tunic. But then again, what would I go swimming in? "I can't stand this outfit," I said. I took the top piece of the tunic off and folded it.

"You'll get used to it," Deon said. "It is actually quite comfort-able once you do. I tried wearing jeans and clothes from your world and find them very uncomfortable and constricting."

"Well I feel like a girl," I told them. "And it makes me uncomfortable all the time."

"And in your world," Oaren replied, "you might be embar-rassed to wear a tunic. But here, that is the style. And especially the one you have because it was designed for Prince Jedrick."

"It was?" gasped Kristjana.

"Yes," said Oaren. "The tailor said that she had designed the outfits she gave to Trey for Jedrick and that Jedrick and Trey are about the same size."

"That's incredible," said Kristjana. "Do you know how special that is?"

"I get it," I was a little short with her. "I just want to stop focusing on my royalty and start focusing on finding Aerian."

They sat, silent, staring at me. I wasn't happy with myself for being so short but at the same time, sometimes that's the only way to actually accomplish anything.

"I'm going to put this in my room," I told them, showing them the top of the tunic. "Then I'm going to head out to the river and see if that gives me any clues as to where Aerian could be."

"I need your help in the field," Deon told Oaren as I left the room. I could tell they were ready to change the subject as well.

When I got to my room, I sat down on the bed. It was as uncomfortable to sit on as it was to sleep on but I was finally alone. I now had time to digest what had happened in the city. I accomplished everything I had set out to do but, in the process, the Knights of the Abyss discovered that I'm on the island. It would be only a matter of time until they found me and tried to kill me. I still had to save Aerian and figure out how to help the island as a whole. And I also wanted to try to find my real parents.

Voices came through the window from outside. I stood up, walked to the window, and opened it. The air was cooler than earlier and it provided a much needed freshness to the room. I inhaled deeply which allowed me to relax.

Deon talked to a large man in a white tunic. I couldn't see the man's face but I saw that he had black hair. Oaren seemed to be uncomfortable and stood a step behind his father, who stood in front of the large man.

"It is not good, Deon," said the large man in a deep voice.

"I understand," Deon replied. "We expected this would happ-en when we first heard the news of the royal family being murdered."

"This has nothing to do with the murders," the man said. "This is because the Knights of the Abyss know that a royal is on the island and there are people helping him. They will kill anyone who is involved with the new prince."

Oaren took a few steps back. I watched Deon's head turn and look at Oaren. "Go inside," Deon told him. Oaren moved quickly toward the house.

"I heard the Knights will address the island soon," the man continued. "They are supposed to impose new laws about conspiracies, traitors, and helping the enemy. Rumor is that they are going to put a reward out for the death of the new Prince and for anyone who is caught helping him. They said they are going to offer money to those who turn in the traitors."

"I would never turn anyone in," said Deon. "They killed the royal family. They are going to destroy this island."

"They are going to kill us if we don't side with them," the man reasoned. "If I know of anyone helping the Prince, I will turn him or her in. Besides, I could use the money."

"Money is not everything," Deon said.

"There is talk of a civilian revolution," the man said. "If a war breaks out between civilians and the Knights, I want to be on the right side."

"And the right side would be?" Deon asked.

"The Knights, of course. I already told you I don't want to cross them."

"I agree that there will be a war," Deon said. "And that it is important to make sure we are on the right side. I'm not sure I agree with your choice though. The Knights want supreme rule over the land. They will scrutinize our lives from how much money we make to how much food we have."

"Trey," Oaren interrupted my focus, "get away from the window."

I stepped back and turned to face him. "Who is that guy?" I asked.

"He lives in a house not far from here and he thinks the Knights are going to ask the Atlanteans to help find you and kill you."

"Do you think they will?"

"Some..." Oaren's eyes showed concern. I could tell he was deep in thought, probably about the fact that his family helped me and now they could be moments away from death. "...I think that the island will be split. There are always some people that listen to the uprisers, no matter how bad their beliefs are. If the Knights promise money and protection, people will take their word for it. They will not question them until it is too late and the Knights will already have control of the island."

I thought about his statements for a moment. He was right. Many horrible things could've been prevented in the history of the world if people would've just questioned their leaders. If only people were brave enough to stand up to those they felt were more powerful than themselves.

"Then I guess it's my job to help the Atlanteans feel like they have a chance to question and stand against the Knights," I said.

"That is what I have been saying all this time," Oaren told me. "But I think you already started that. The man said some things that made me believe that our revolution is already in progress. We can go downstairs and see what is going on.

I followed Oaren downstairs and we went to the living room. Oaren put his hand on the panel of water that functions like a television. The panel of water lit up and the island of Atlantis appeared. He took his index finger and ran it down the screen causing the image to zoom in. Within seconds, we saw crowds of people shouting at the Knights of the Abyss.

"Exactly as I predicted," Oaren said. "The uprising is in progress, thanks to you."

"What are they angry about?" I asked. An old man screaming at a Knight answered my question. The old man complained of laws that would take away their privacy if the Knights enforced them. The Knight argued back that it is for the safety of the island. I heard hatred, fear, and anger in the Atlantean language for the first time.

"You killed a shop owner because you suspected that they helped our new prince," said a middle-aged woman with graying hair.

"Traitors deserve to be punished," the Knight countered.

I looked at Oaren; his eyes reinforced the fact that he thought the same thing I did. Someone we encountered today was dead. Was it the tailor or the map shop owner?

"He was a map shop owner," the woman continued. "He sold a map that was sold to him and you killed him for it."

"He sold it to an enemy," the Knight told her. "The boy he sold it to is trying to overthrow the government and wants to start a revolution. This will not be allowed. For the safety of the people."

"You are making up stories," the woman replied. "There is no boy. That is just an excuse to go around killing people."

"I do not need an excuse to do anything," the Knight told her. He pushed her with all his might. The woman fell backwards and tumbled head over heels to the ground. Her head bounced off the ground and she lay motionless. "Afti entasi prepei telos!"

"This tension just ended," Oaren translated to English as I made the translation in my head.

"Gia esy echo agathos," the Knight added.

The crowd chanted; loud, clear, and serious. *Katadioxi. Katapiezo.* The words created butterflies in my stomach. I was responsible for this. I needed to act on this. I was the one that needed to harness this frustration and use it to save the island from oppression.

The Knights used force to disperse the crowds as much as possible. And then the word that said it all echoed above the crowd. *Adikia.* It rang in my ears like someone had shouted it as loud as they could, as if they were only inches from me.

"That's what I was hoping for," Oaren said. "That is the word I was waiting for. Nothing causes people to act more than a feeling of injustice."

Deon's entrance in the room interrupted our focus on the screen. His eyes showed concern as he took in the scene we were watching. Kristjana followed and I saw fear. My heart and stomach wrenched as the man that Deon had talked to outside, the one that said he would tell the Knights if he knew where I was, entered the room.

His dark eyes met mine. I could read his thoughts from his expression. He would find a way to contact the Knights and report me. He looked at Deon with shock and then to Kristjana. "How could you harbor a criminal?"

"Criminal?" Oaren said. "He is not the one that murdered the royal family. He is here to save our island."

"How dare you insult our rulers," the man spat.

"They are no more our rulers than you are," Deon said. "And we are proud to provide a safe harbor for our new Prince."

The man looked at Deon. "Prodotis!"

Deon stared back with conviction. He didn't budge at the accusation of being a traitor.

The man looked at Kristjana and shouted, "Mourntaria!" He turned to Oaren. "Leronero!"

"How dare you?!," Deon growled in anger. "Get out of our house!"

"With pleasure," the man said. He started to leave, stopped, and turned to us. "The Knights will hear about you filthy traitors who thought it was acceptable to harbor a criminal."

"Get out!" Deon moved toward the man. The man took the warning and scurried out of the house.

The room remained silent but the exchanged looks said it all. Things were changing fast for all of us. The island was on the brink of civil war and now neighbors were reporting other neighbors to garner rewards.

"We have to find Aerian," I said, pushing all else to the side.

"Alright," Kristjana said, "you go to the river and try to con-nect with her. We will start packing. We are not going to be able to stay here long now that the neighbor is going to alert the Knights."

"Right," I agreed. I looked at the three faces around me. They were going to have to run because they were helping me. They were going to have to abandon their house, leave everything behind, because of me. As much as I wished I could just end this and go home to the life I knew, I realized that life didn't exist anymore. I couldn't leave this family now that they were targeted as traitors. "We're in it for the long haul," I said. "Whatever we do, we have to make it fast."

SYNDESI

I ran, as fast as I could, up the steps to my room. I went straight to the cloth bag the woman in the tailor shop had packed for me. Inside, I found the other tunics and boots.

I took the bag and went back downstairs and handed it to Oaren. "Make sure this is with the stuff to go with us." Then I pulled the sword from the sheath on my belt and handed it to Oaren, followed by the map I had in my belt.

"Got it," he told me.

"I'll make this quick," I told them. "Be ready to leave as soon as I get back from the river."

"My mom is packing now," Oaren said.

Without saying anything else, I left the house. The sun sank to the horizon behind me as I ran east, across the fields, toward the river where the family's aftokinero rested. There was no timetable to tell me when the Knights would show up at the house. There was no way of knowing whether it would be minutes or hours before they came looking to murder me and the family that harbored me.

But if we had to run, why not make sure we were looking for Aerian while fleeing from the Knights. That would happen, if I could just figure out where Aerian was being held captive. I hoped that, like the pool allowed me to see Aerian calling for help, the river would connect me to her and show me where she was.

I made it to the river and stared at the smooth flowing liquid. Though I didn't know how or why, the answers I searched for were probably in the water I was about to enter. I untied my belt, let it fall to the ground, and unhooked the tunic bottom from my waist and let it fall. The blue boxers that I got from the tailor were all that covered me as I climbed into the cool, clean water. I held the pendant of my necklace, remembering that Oaren told me it was made of hydrome, as I submerged myself fully in the river.

The necklace sparkled with light and then the light grew stronger, diffusing through the sunlit water. An image appeared in the light emanating from the necklace. Within seconds, I watched it as though it happened live in front of me.

Two Knights of the Abyss were dragging Aerian away from the pool of water. Each one pulled an arm and over powered the little resistance she gave them. She didn't have the energy to fight back. Her face pale; her eyes exhausted.

They moved into the palace and through a number of hallways. I couldn't keep track of which way they turned each time they came to a new hallway but I tried. There were just too many hallways and they turned too many times. They went down steps, many steps, into a darker area of the palace, lit only by candlelight from lanterns on the walls.

Aerian's eyes were barely open as the Knights all but carried her deep-er into the palace. Finally, after descending two more flights of stairs and making numerous turns down completely dark hallways, they came upon a prison cell. The Knights chained Aerian to the wall in the cell and then one of them took a thin piece of wood, let it catch on fire at the only burning lantern, and lit four other lanterns in the room

The Knights stood staring at her, as though she would be able

to put up resistance. But her weakened body was no match for the thick metal chains, which were probably made of hydrome. Unable to keep her head up, Aerian collapsed so that the only thing keeping her from falling to the floor were the chains attached to each wrist.

"Where is the artifact?" said the Knight that lit the lanterns. He placed himself directly in front of the exhausted sorceress. His eyes stared at her with hatred and frustration. Her eyes remained closed, her chin to her chest, body dangling. Aerian didn't respond.

The Knight put one hand on each side of her face and lifted her head so that her closed eyes met with his dark, evil eyes that bore through her. "Where is it?" he yelled. "Open your eyes!"

Aerian's eyelids parted slightly, forced to do so by what appeared to be the last amount of strength she had. The Knight held her face tightly, his eyes locked on hers. "WHERE IS IT?" his voice seemed to shake the room.

"You...will...never...know," said Aerian in an almost inaudible whisper.

"AAAHHH," the Knight cried out in frustration. He released her face, her eyes closed again, and her entire body fell into the hold of the chains.

"What are we going to do?" asked the other Knight.

"Stay here and stand guard. I am going to search her room and she better hope that I find it or else I will be back for further interrogation. If I find it, I will let her death be quick and as painless as possible." The Knights left the cell. The one that was ordered to stand guard locked the cell door while the other left the room.

The scene went dark and my focus was back on the river. Rocks littered the floor. A creature, that looked like a crayfish, crawled under a rock with a tiny minnow in its claw. The pain in my lungs brought my mind back to reality. I needed air. I shot out of the river and gasped.

My lungs expanded and then contracted, saturating the blood with the oxygen needed to revitalize my body. I gasped a few more breaths.

The scene that I just watched had not been live. I saw Aerian at the pond in my vision two days ago. There was no way that it took the Knights that long to find and detain her. Though I didn't know how the connection worked, I was glad she left me a vision of where they took her. I now knew she was in a cell in the deep dungeon of the palace. I didn't know where that dungeon was specifically but at least I had a start.

I studied the environment around me. No one was near the river. Figuring I had time, I submerged myself in the water again, hoping to see another vision, one that would give me a better idea of where Aerian was held captive. Once again, the light infiltrated the water and formed an image.

The dungeon containing the cell with the young sorceress was now dark, barely lit by one tiny flame on a candle on the wall in a corner of the room. Aerian still hung limply, chained to the wall. Large cuffs connected her to thick chains that held her captive. She appeared to be more coherent than in the last vision.

Voices faded in and then two Knights entered the vision. One had fire in his eyes that bore a hole through Aerian as he walked toward her, his breathing agitated.

"Where is the boy?" the Knight asked.

Aerian didn't respond.

The Knight's eyes filled with even more anger. He ground his teeth, "Where...is...the...boy?"

Aerian ignored him again.

"Make this easier on yourself," the Knight said. "Tell me where he is."

"I do not know who you are talking about," Aerian said.

"The boy you were looking at in the Mnemosunero," the Knight replied. "The one who thinks he is the new prince."

"You are mistaken," Aerian said.

"Mistaken," the Knight spit with anger. "I know what you saw."

"Then why do you need me to fill you in?" Aerian asked.

The Knight placed his face close to hers and put a hand on her cheek, forcing her to stare into his eyes. "I am not playing games with you. There is a boy, you saw him in the Mnemosunero, and he thinks he is the new Prince. Now he is on this island and we came across him in the city. We need to know where he is."

Aerian thought about it for a minute and then answered. "I do not know where he is now. I do not have the connection with him without the Mnemosunero."

"How did he get the necklace?!" the Knight asked, still hold-ing her face in front of his own.

"What necklace?"

The Knight squeezed her face tight. Aerian cringed with pain. "The necklace that belongs to Atlantean royalty. The one that makes this poor, unfortunate boy our new Prince."

"For now," added the other Knight.

"Once again, I do not know what you are talking about."

"AAAHHH," the Knight screamed as he pushed Aerian's head away from him and spun on his feet, turning the opposite direction. He paced away from her, still groaning in anger, and then turned and walked back to her.

"Your anger does not suit your purpose," said Aerian. "I am used to working with the royal family who never..."

"The royal family is dead," the Knight spat in her face. "When will you and the people of this island realize that times have changed? If you want your life to continue to be worth living, you will tell me where the boy is and how he received the necklace."

"Actually," said Aerian, "if I want to live a good, long life, I will keep that secret to myself."

"What makes you so sure that the boy is a savior for this island? Why are you certain he is special?"

"Because I know who he is," Aerian said. "I know what is in his blood. And I know that he knows where you are holding me captive."

"How does he know?"

"Main river, fourth grate on the left, three floors down, second door on the left."

"What are you rambling about?" The Knight stared at Aerian with frustration. The same frustration I saw in my Dad's eyes when he took me to the hospital to find out why I had visions during the swim meet.

"The boy will stop you."

Another Knight entered the dungeon room. "We have information that might lead us to the boy. A farmer reported that a family near his house is harboring the boy."

"See the key," Aerian whispered when she realized they weren't listening to her any more. "Follow my directions and use the map."

She knew we were connected now. I wanted to talk to her, find out more about where they were keeping her.

"You must go," she continued. "Danger is approaching fast."

The Knights turned their attention back to her. "I am going to ask you one more time," said the Knight that was interrogating her the entire time. "Where is the boy and how did he get the necklace?"

"I am going to tell you one more time," Aerian said with confidence. "I do not know!"

The Knight backhanded her, leaving a red handprint on her right cheek. I wanted to help her but I was nowhere near her. She brought her head back to face the Knight again. Her eyes were filled with tears, her face with anger.

"Even Atlas would not have done that," said Aerian.

The Knight backhanded her again, harder this time. "Which is why we are better rulers than Atlas. We do not take any nonsense." While Aerian was trying to fight the pain, the Knight turned to the one that most recently entered the dungeon room. "Where are our riders?"

"On their way to the farms," answered the Knight.

Aerian's eyes opened, fear exploding from them. "RUN!!!" she screamed.

I realized that she was talking to me when the connection ended with a sharp pain on my scalp. The image turned to bright light, fading completely in seconds. Another tug on my hair caused more pain to my scalp. I pushed my hands at whatever was holding my hair and realized, quickly, that it was a hand.

I tried to push the hand away but it yanked on my hair again and pulled my upper body out of the water. A Knight stood in front of me, his gloved hand still clenched on my hair. I tried to punch the Knight but he blocked it with his other arm. He released my hair and pushed me backwards with all of his might. My back crashed off the rocks on the bottom of the river.

Ignoring the pain, I struggled to my feet. The bank of the river was a few feet from me so I headed toward it. The Knight splashed behind me, following in my footsteps. As I climbed onto the bank, my only thought was about making it to the house to warn Oaren and his family. But then the horrible fear crossed my mind. What if the Knights already found them while they were waiting for me to get back from the river?

A lasso caught my foot as I ran and I crashed face down, hard, on the ground. The hit made the air rush out of my lungs and I gasped to take more in. I struggled as the rope drug me toward the Knight pulling on it with all his might. I grasped at the rope around my ankle, trying to loosen it but found no success.

My feet at his ankles, he reached down to grab me and I did everything in my power to keep him from gaining an advantage. I scratched, slapped, punched, kicked, kneed, and even tried to bite him as he fought to get control of me. If only I had my sword, but I'd handed it to Oaren along with the map.

I kicked his kneecap and, with a crunch, his knee gave out and he fell to the ground. I took the opportunity, since the Knight was no longer holding the rope, to climb to my feet and run. The rope, that just moments ago bound me to the Knight, was now trailing behind me. I ran toward the house. I had to get help, if the family was still there and unharmed. And, if they were in trouble, I had to help them.

I approached the house, slowing my pace and observing cautiously. The last thing I wanted to do was walk into a trap. I stopped about four feet from the door and removed the rope as I heard Oaren talking inside. He didn't sound like he was stressed or troubled in anyway, so I entered the house.

"I was attacked," I yelled. "We have to go now." I put my hand out, "I need my sword."

The fear on Oaren's face told me everything before he spoke. The Knights were in the house. The family was trying to make it look like I wasn't around; I just made a potentially fatal mistake. I stared in Oaren's eyes, allowed mine to ask him where the Knights were. He gestured his head up.

My heart, which now felt like it was going to burst out of my chest, seemed to miss a few beats when the Knight came around the corner from the kitchen. My mind was blank. The fight or flight mechanism should have kicked in but it didn't.

"Give me my sword," I said to Oaren again. I still didn't have a plan, but at least I would have some protection with the sword in my possession. Oaren shook his head 'no' and then guided his eyes to a blanket on the floor in the corner of the room.

The Knight's eyes pierced through me. I knew it wouldn't be long until he attacked me and I thought about how I was going to get the sword from under the blanket fast enough.

"Did you give them the map?" I questioned, strategically. "That's all they are looking for. Just give it to them and they'll go away." I pretended that I didn't know they were after me.

"I thought you had the map," Oaren played along. He used his eyes to show me that the map was with the sword under the blanket.

"I put it over here," I said as I started to walk toward the corner where the sword was laying, hidden, under the blanket. "Let me just get it for you and you can be on your way," I added, looking at the Knight and smiling.

"I'm not here for the map," he replied. "Although I will take the map with me." He made his move toward me and I threw myself at the blanket on the floor. I landed on my stomach at the edge of the blanket, slid my hand under it, and grabbed the sword. The Knight came at me and I swung the sword out from under the blanket and sliced at him. He was quick enough to back out of the way.

I climbed to my feet as the Knight prepared himself to battle me by pulling his sword out of its scabbard. In a defensive stance, I carefully watched for his next move. Oaren stood behind him, his face frozen in fear. It was only after I watched navy blue collapse to the floor and a puddle of red form that I realized why Oaren was staring in fear. Deon had taken a sword and stabbed the Knight in the back. Oaren watched his father murder someone. It could not have been easy to do. But what choice did Deon have.

"Get out of the house," Deon said, pointing for me to leave through the door. "You too, Oaren." Deon looked at his son. Oaren was still frozen with the same expression of shock. "Go," Deon reiterated, "before the others come and it is too late."

"Come on," I called for Oaren to follow me after grabbing the map. He looked at his dad and then grabbed the bag with my clothes and walked toward the door. We moved regretfully, but quickly, at having to leave the house. I hoped that Deon and Kristjana, wherever she was, would follow us soon.

"Kristjana," I heard Deon call for her. "Come on, we're leaving."

And then, like the shot heard round the world, came the words of the Knights.

"Prodotis," a Knight yelled, "fonias". Outside the house, it was as clear as if we were standing in front of them.

What happened next, though we only observed through sounds, changed everything. The yells of anger. The specific, reputation-damaging words connected with foul words being thrown at the two people that took me in. And then the blood-curdling cry of Kristjana as Deon screamed in pain. Deon's scream ended quickly. Then, within moments, Kristjana's blood curdling cry of horror and sadness turned to that of pain, until it faded away into oblivion.

The Knights were now going to come for us. I grabbed Oaren by the arm and pulled him, practically dragging him toward the forest. Once we were in the forest, hidden by the outer most trees, I stopped and allowed myself to digest what happened. I stared at Oaren.

His face was blank; his eyes were empty. It was obvious that our entire world had changed. This game of revolution and standing up against the Knights had just taken a turn for reality. Oaren's life was never going to be the same and mine, through association, would be different as well. And I was now absolutely certain that my life was forever shattered and I was going to have to get used to facing the challenges brought on by my new destiny.

Ries

Oaren collapsed into a squat, close to the ground after we had walked less than a half-mile into the woods. After a few moments of sobbing into his hands, hiding his face from me, he crumpled even further so that he was now sitting against a tree. The dense foliage from the trees caused the world around us to be darker than it should have been at this time of day.

Oaren hadn't said a word the entire time we were walking. I figured he wasn't up for talking so I didn't say anything either. I had never dealt with the death of someone close to me, let alone my parents. But I figured at some point, he was going to have to take a moment to let the shock and emotion out and begin to realize the ramifications of what had happened. On the other hand, I didn't want to deal with the ramifications.

Wasn't I the reason his parents were dead? If I hadn't allowed them to take me in, they wouldn't have been killed. If I hadn't come back from the city, they wouldn't be dead. Maybe if I hadn't run when the Knights were in the house, I would be dead but they would be alive. I didn't want to face these truths. And I certainly didn't want to face Oaren when he started to face these truths.

Beyond this particular issue, which was a huge one, there was the issue of still having to locate Aerian and save her from the Knights. Plus, the Knights were still going to hunt me and I knew, more now than ever, that they would kill anyone to get to me. And there was also the task of trying to locate my biological family and figure out my origins.

Oaren was on the ground, his face in his hands, sobbing hysterically. The shock wore off. The emotions were no longer contained. Though we hadn't talked since his parents met their fate, I knew that he was trying to make sense of everything that happened. I knew that he was trying to connect all of the pieces; trying to figure out if somehow, someway, the death of his parents could have been prevented.

I already knew that answer. Their deaths could have been prevented. Had I not met them, his parents would still be alive. Sooner or later, that fact was going to be something that Oaren would have to deal with. And, even though I was already dealing with that fact, I was going to have to deal with it when he dealt with it. That was an uncomfortable thought.

But at the moment, he was grieving for his parents. I had no way of knowing what that was like. Sure I lost my family just a couple of days ago but they were still alive. I could see them if I wanted to. That wasn't an option for Oaren.

I stared at Oaren and I felt helpless. I didn't know what to say to him. I didn't know how to help him. All I could do was show him that I cared. I walked over to him and knelt down so that I was level with him. His face was still buried in his hands, the sniffling told me he was still crying. I figured that if I'd lost both my parents, even if they were only my adopted parents, I wouldn't be able to stop crying for days. They were the two people that raised me and helped me become who I am today.

In a gesture to show that I cared and that I was there for anything he needed, I placed my hand on his right shoulder. Oaren picked his head up out of his hands and stared at me. His sadness turned to fury as he pushed my arm away. Then he pushed me and I fell backwards, landing on my back, staring at him in shock.

Oaren climbed to his feet and I did the same. "You," he cried. "This is all your fault. My parents are dead because you came here."

"I…" I tried to respond but I didn't know how. And even if I did have the words, I wouldn't have been able to get them out fast enough, Oaren pushed me again. I stumbled backwards and bumped into a tree.

"This is your fault," he continued to let his frustrations be known. "You caused this!" He pushed at me again but I had nowhere to go because the tree behind me was supporting me.

"I'm sorry," I told him. It was the only thing I could say. I knew this was coming but I didn't expect it this fast. I thought I would have time to figure out a response before it came to this.

"You are sorry?" he cried. "Sorry? You do not even know what that word means. You do not know what it is like to lose your parents. And for what? They are dead because some wannabe prince comes looking to save the day. They are dead because some wannabe prince had visions of a pretty girl in trouble. You want to rescue your damsel in distress, do you? Well go ahead but leave me out of it."

I didn't know how to respond to him. I came to Atlantis because I had visions of Aerian calling for help. But there was more to it than that. My real parents were here on the island. I was an Atlantean. And I was, for some reason, the one that was supposed to stop the Knights of the Abyss.

Besides, Oaren and his parents were the ones that found me. I didn't go to them for help; they came looking for me. And they were the ones that offered to help me and put their lives and reputations on the line. I didn't ask for that. But I didn't think I should tell him any of that.

He was making statements based on emotion. He wasn't thinking. His body chemistry was getting the best of him and causing him to act based on his sadness and anger. He wanted someone to blame and so his mind was giving him someone to blame, even if it wasn't the right person.

Oaren pushed me again, harder this time. Still, there was nowhere for me to go. The force caused my back to smash against the trunk of the large tree. "I hate you," he cried. Tears streamed from his eyes like a raging river. "You are nothing more than a wannabe prince. You could never lead this island. You ruined my life. I want nothing to do with you. I am leaving and I do not want to ever see you again. I... hate... you..."

Something I didn't expect happened. Anger and hurt started to boil in my blood. My jaws clenched and I felt my muscles contract. I'll show him a wannabe prince! I didn't even want this.

I didn't ask for it. My life was ruined too.

If there is one thing that proves to be a problem with adole-scent boys, it's that your testosterone won't let someone else's testosterone get the best of you. Oaren turned to walk away but, before he could, I jumped him and tackled him to the ground. He groaned and mumbled in Atlantean but the words were not clear enough for me to understand what he was saying. He pushed at my face as I, leaning over him, held him down. I was in control.

"Get off me," he yelled. He tried hitting my face but I captur-ed both of his arms and pressed them down on the ground with my own.

"Take it back," I told him.

"Never," he said. "You are the reason my parents are dead."

I leaned my knees on him and put more pressure on his arms. "I came here to save this island. I came here because Aerian called me. I didn't ask for this. And I certainly didn't ask for your help, or your parents' help for that matter. You came to me, remember?"

"We helped you because you could never rule this island without our help! And we needed someone to lead us. Unfortunately, you were our only choice."

"That doesn't say a lot for you and the people of Atlantis," I countered.

Oaren rallied his strength, pushed his arms against mine, and was able to uproot me and practically knock me off of him. He used one more burst of strength to take advantage of my already compromised position and pushed me completely off of him. And within seconds, we were rolling around in the dirt, pushing at each other with our arms and legs.

Oaren rolled me onto my stomach, my face pressing into the ground. He knelt on me, knees holding my arms behind my back. His hands were on the back of my head, pressing my face into the soil. I spit to keep the dirt out of my mouth and fought to breathe anything but the fine dust of the dry soil.

My body was scratched, soon to be bruised. My boxers only protected a small area of my skin from being damaged in the fight. The flesh of my face, arms, legs, chest, stomach, and back was ripped and sore from the rocks and twigs on the ground we had just rolled over.

The assault ended. Even though I was held captive, unable to move, my fury had diminished. Oaren seemed to have calmed himself as well.

And then I heard the sniffling again and, a few moments later, I felt some tears land on my upper back.

He released the pressure he had on me and I was able to move

my arms and face again. Oaren collapsed on me and then rolled off and lay, sobbing, on the ground next to me. I moved myself into a sitting position and wiped the dirt from my face as best I could.

I looked at Oaren. His body was scratched and bleeding, like mine. The dirt on his face had turned darker and clumped into mud from the tears streaming from his eyes. The bottom of his tunic was wrinkled, dirty, and had a few small holes in it. We were both going to need new clothes.

I felt awkward and vulnerable. I could deal with being in a swimsuit for the swim meets but it was something about being in my boxers in the middle of the woods, on an unfamiliar island, with a boy a little younger than me that made being so uncovered not appropriate and disturbing to one's mind. I could only imagine what the guys on my swim team would say, especially if they saw me wrestling with Oaren just a few minutes ago.

Our fight seemed so senseless now. Embarrassed by the fact that I allowed my emotions to get the best of me, my mind reprimanded itself for not dealing with the situation in a more responsible, mature way. Oaren's mind was compromised by the emotions and the chemistry in his body brought on by those emotions. Even though that was what happened with me, it was not an excuse. His emotions were brought on by the tragic loss of those close to him. Mine were brought on by damage to my boyish pride. It was disgusting that I allowed it to turn into a wrestling match.

Maybe Oaren was right. I wasn't fit to lead these people. I couldn't even manage to deal with a little hurt pride. I had no idea what it was like to deal with a real challenge. Even Oaren had that experience over me. I really was just a wannabe prince.

A loud snap switched my mind from thought to search and my eyes and ears scoped the environment around me. A twig? Perhaps an animal stepped on one on the ground. Or maybe a squirrel or a bird caused one to snap in the trees above. Did they even have squirrels or birds in Atlantis? I couldn't remember if I had seen any since I got here. Of course that didn't mean that there weren't any. I wasn't always the most observant person.

Before I could ponder the situation any longer, I saw move-ment; navy blue cloth swiped quickly past a large bush.

"The Knights," Oaren yelled.

No time to react. At least ten Knights emerged from the dense trees and bushes around us. My sword was feet away, next to a tree where I had dropped it at the start of the scuffle with Oaren.

"Kill the Prince," hissed the Knight standing directly in front of me. The Knights rushed at me, their swords aiming to kill. I had no protection at all so I just closed my eyes and tried to cover myself with my arms, just an instinct, it wouldn't do any good.

Metal clanged on metal and the Knights yelled in anger as more metal collided. I opened my eyes. Atlantean soldiers battled with the Knights. The metal clanging was loud and made me realize that I should probably get my sword and try to help. I saw the soldier from the city that saved us from the Knights when they had Oaren corned outside the store. He directed the other soldiers, working the logistics of how to defeat the Knights.

I ran to my sword, grabbed it, and then studied the surround-ing battle. I got my sword just in time; a Knight came at me, slashing his sword. I blocked his blade with mine and our swords stayed together, like magnets. The Knight pushed on his sword and caused me to stumble backwards.

I pulled my sword away from his and gripped it tighter. I raised it over my head at the perfect moment to block his from attempting to slice me in half. I used my sword to push him backwards, my strength was just enough to take him off guard. I repositioned my sword and swiped it at his feet. He jumped over the blade and then swung his sword at my head. I ducked, just low enough to avoid the blade, but I felt the breeze of the sword on my hair.

He swiped his sword at me again. I blocked it. Again and I blocked it. The next time our swords met, he maneuvered it in a way that I couldn't predict. I lost my grip and control of my sword and he knocked it out of my hands with his own weapon, sending it flying a few feet away. Not wasting any time, he slashed at me in all directions with all of his might. I jumped out of the way, ducked, and jumped out of the way again.

I avoided the blade for some time, until he trapped me against a large tree trunk. Only his eyes were exposed but I could tell that he was enjoying this. He was going to get credit for killing the new Prince.

I watched the shiny blade raise into the air. I saw my own reflection in the smooth, clean metal. The tip of the blade pointed right between my eyes. There was only one way to possibly avoid death and I waited for it. I had to be precise with the only thing that would save my life.

The blade tip raced towards me as fast as the Knight could push it. I didn't close my eyes; instead, I watched it very closely. I calculated the exact moment and then I ducked. I heard the blade pierce the tree trunk. I ducked out from between the Knight and the tree. The Knight pulled on the sword with all his might but it

was stuck in the tree.

The Knight gave up and left the blade lodged in the trunk. He turned to me and now I saw only fury in his eyes. The joy of killing me was stolen from him and he wasn't happy. I outsmarted him and, sword or no sword, he wasn't going to let that go.

My sword laid just a few feet from me. I moved for it but the Knight already expected me to do that. He dove in front of me, catching me with his massive arms. I fought to break free but was unsuccessful. My arms were useless, thanks to the fact that his arms wrapped around me like a boa constrictor.

He lifted me into the air, I kicked as hard as I could, but found myself unable to connect with the Knight's body. He tossed me to the ground and I landed on my right side. Hard. Pain shot through my right shoulder and arm. I rubbed it with my left hand, trying to ease the pain enough to fight back.

The Knight stalked toward me like a lion about to go for the kill on a helpless baby antelope. I pushed myself, painfully, backwards trying to put more distance between the Knight and myself.

"Fun time is over, boy," the Knight growled. He didn't have a sword, neither did I, but I knew that he could kill me without one. His arms were certainly powerful enough to strangle me. He screamed as he lunged. I saw a blur dive at his legs.

Oaren took out the Knight's legs. The Knight landed on his left foot, his body weight crushing down on him. I heard the snap of his ankle as I ran for my sword. The Knight screamed in pain but didn't waste any time climbing back to his feet. He threw himself at Oaren, putting his entire body weight into knocking Oaren down. Oaren flew a few feet before crashing to the ground. I dove toward my sword and grabbed it.

The Knight came toward me, as though nothing happened to his ankle. He lunged and I pushed the sword out in front of me and closed my eyes. I felt the collision; heard the piercing of flesh. The high pitched whimper of air rushing out of the Knight made me open my eyes. The sword was in his stomach.

I pulled the sword out and gasped in disgust, shock, and fear as the Knight fell on me and his blood poured onto my body. I fought to get out from under the heavy body and then sat up. Two Knights ran away and a few soldiers followed them. The other seven Knights laid motionless on the ground.

The soldier from the city met my eyes with his. His chest heaved from the exertion of the battle. His armor, and the tunic under it, were stained with blood, which I assumed was not his own.

He nodded his approval at me. "I'm Ries," he told me, still catching his breath. Oaren helped me up and then stood at my side.

"I'm Trey," I replied.

"And I'm Oaren."

"Well my Prince," Ries said. "You did alright. But you'll need some training if you are going to lead our revolution."

I looked at him, feeling a mixture of exhaustion, fear, and pain; my shoulder was still killing me. I rubbed my shoulder and decided to break the tension with a joke. "Well, in my defense, there's not much need for learning to sword fight in a Miami high school."

Ries ignored my comment. "Get your sword and clean it. We're going to set up camp. I collected enough Atlantean soldiers to protect you. We'll keep watch over camp and you'll get some rest. We need to start training first thing in the morning."

I looked at Oaren. He looked as tired and emotionally wrought as I felt. Overwhelmed with emotion, he needed some time to deal with the events forced on him by the day. And, as tired as I was, I didn't think I would be able to sleep. I had enough things to comprehend. Oaren's parents were killed because of me. And I killed for the first time today, twice in fact. Killing two human beings was not something I wanted to, nor was I prepared to deal with, even if it was in self-defense.

NYKTERINOS

I needed to wash off in the river. I could not rest until I washed the dirt and dried blood from my body. The fact that someone's blood was on me made me ill. Ries accepted my request and ordered one of his soldiers to accompany me to the river. He said it was necessary, for my protection.

I agreed and, shortly after we had everything settled for the night, I headed to the river with a soldier that looked to be in his late twenties. His short, light brown hair was unstyled. Now in a seaweed green tunic, I noticed the jellyfish tattoo on his right arm. Medousa. The symbol of the military.

We made it to the river in just a few minutes. This particular spot was as much forest as the spot where camp was set up. The river weaved its way through the trees, the large trunks and roots grew right on the bank. Dark night had set in while we set up camp. The foliage over the river blocked out the moonlight, except for small patches where there were no leaves.

The soldier started to say something in Atlantean and then stopped. He switched to English and said, "I'll stand guard here on the bank."

I didn't care to make sure they knew I understood Atlantean. That secret might be the very one that would mean life or death because, if they thought I didn't understand Atlantean, they might talk about things I should know about. For example, I didn't yet know if I could trust Ries and the rest of the soldiers.

How could I make the decision to trust them? With the exception of Ries, none of the other soldiers introduced themselves to me. I couldn't be too careful. Anyone on the island could be a Knight of the Abyss. And besides that, some people, like Oaren's neighbor, were going to side with the Knights in order to protect themselves.

The water rushed by as I stood on the bank between two large trees. Flowing faster than in the other sections, I figured it would be easier to wash off. I carefully climbed down the bank and lowered myself into the water. One last look at the environment around me reinforced that darkness was concealing it. The

soldier's outline stood guard on the bank.

My body floated into relaxation. The force of the water wash-ed the dirt off of me. The cool water was a comfort to the aches from the day. I submerged in the water so that I could wash my face and hair.

A scream. A flash of bright light. Another scream. A flash of a vision I couldn't make out. Another scream. It was Aerian's scream. *The flashing pictures flew through my mind in a blur. Images of Aerian in chains, being assaulted by the Knights, were interrupted by blackness.*

This was much different than the previous visions of Aerian. Something was wrong with the connection. The Knights were hurting her; they were keeping her mind from making the connection.

Aerian!

Trey. The vision was less interrupted now. Like a faulty movie projector continuously fading out and then back in.

I focused harder to pick up every little piece of the vision I could. *I saw Aerian, still chained to the wall in a dimly lit, concrete room. She struggled to get free as four Knights approached her.* The vision went black and I realized I needed oxygen. I shot out of the water and gulped in air.

"Esy blepe entaxei?" the soldier asked from the riverbank.

"I'm fine," I answered and then re-submerged. I wasn't lying to him, I was fine. In fact, I was better than I had been all day. Except I was kicking myself for letting it slip that I understood Atlantean. And I was also worried that I couldn't say that Aerian was alright.

The vision reappeared. A Knight smacked Aerian across the face and the picture went to black for a few seconds. When it came back, the Knight mumbled something unclear in Atlantean. Aerian screamed a very defiant "oche" in his face.

He smacked her again and the picture cut out for another moment. It faded back in. "Bazo telos se," he hissed fury at her. "Opou einai o orasi?"

Tell him where the 'sight' is I instructed her with my mind. He said he will put a stop to this.

"No!" she cried. "They cannot know!"

"Afti einai syndesi maz ton," the Knight turned toward the others. "Tyranno tis mechri afti milo."

NO!!!

Do not come for me! That is what they want.

They're going to torture you.

Forget me. You are more important, my Prince.

The Knight slapped her again and the picture cut out but only for a

second. He looked right into Aerian's eyes so that I could stare into his. He laughed evilly. "Erchomai mou Basilias." He laughed and then hit her harder than all the other times.

The vision cut out and didn't come back. I pushed up and out of the water and swam to the bank. I climbed out and sat staring into the river. The soldier walked over to me but didn't say anything.

The Knight, aware of the connection, had definitely taunted me. He said, "Come, my Prince." But even still, he clearly told the other Knights to torture her until she talked. They wanted to know where the 'sight' was. What was the 'sight'?

"We best get back to camp, my Prince," the soldier said.

I agreed and stood up. We started walking back to camp and I realized that the guy that was supposed to protect me was no more than ten years older than me and I didn't even know his name. I didn't know if I should ask for his name. Maybe it was best to just let him do his job and not get to know him, in case something happened.

"My name is Troy," he said.

I freaked out inside. Either he read my mind or he wanted to break up the silence. I didn't know how to respond, since he already knew my name, so I didn't.

"All of the men in my family were soldiers. They were all sworn to protect the ruling families. My dad and grandfather are retired. My brother will serve you as well. He is at the camp with Ries."

I felt the opportunity to get answers to some questions. "Is Ries your leader?"

"Ries is an experienced soldier that wants to stand against the Knights. As you know, it is not clear who are the friends and who are the foes and we are just as confused as you. Ries is gathering up all of the Atlantean military he can to create an opposition against the Knights. My brother and I joined because we want revenge. Our cousin was one of the soldiers that protected the family inside the palace when the Knights infiltrated it and killed just about everyone inside. Not only that but we both liked the royal family and do not want to live under the rule of the Knights. Lucky for us, you are here."

I didn't know how to respond. Could I trust this soldier? I didn't even know him. And even if everything he was saying was true, I still didn't know how I would respond to it. It put me right back in the place I didn't want to be. I was on the island to help Aerian and try to figure out who my real parents were. But the Atlanteans were counting on me to rule their civilization.

How could I deny them that? How could I tell them I wasn't going to lead them? They lost their royal family and some of them lost their blood family in the uprising. There was no one in line to rule this island, except me. If I didn't accept, I would leave them in even more hopelessness and tragedy. But if I did choose to lead them, what did that mean for my life?

Was I fit to lead them? I didn't think so but if most of the people I met today thought so, and Aerian thought so, then maybe I was. Who was I to decide who was fit to rule Atlantis? I looked at Troy.

"You are going to lead us, aren't you?" he asked.

"I don't know yet," I answered honestly. "For now we just have to save Aerian. We have to make our move tonight. She's in trouble."

We entered the camp perimeter. More than a dozen tents sat around the perimeter. One large tent sat in the center. I stopped and took it all in as the soldiers talked about how to protect camp and worked out sleeping shifts.

Ries met us just inside the perimeter of camp. "The tent in the middle is yours, my Prince," he said. "You are the ruling Prince."

"Not yet," I told him.

"You are the ruling Prince," he reiterated. "The civilians of this island do not know it yet but we do. Our job is to protect you at all times. You will never be without a soldier at your side."

"I need to change," I switched the subject, desperately. They treated me like we did our President. They forgot that I was only sixteen and never made any major decisions in my life. "Then we need to figure out how to get in and save Aerian tonight. She's in trouble."

"We are not doing anything tonight except allowing you to rest safely," Ries informed me matter-of-factly. "We are starting your training in the..."

"We can't wait any longer," I cut him off. "Aerian is being tortured. I saw her in a vision when I was in the river. They told her she could stop this if she told them where the 'sight' was."

Ries looked as confused as I felt. "The 'sight'? What is the 'sight'?"

"Are you sure you translated correctly?" Troy asked me.

"That's what I heard," I said. "But I don't know what they're talking about."

"She is a sorceress," Ries said. "You are the ruling Prince. You are more important."

"I'm here because she called me," I raised my voice and forced my hand toward the ground. "I'm here to save her; there's nothing more to it than that. I'm going to save her, with or without your help."

"You will not leave this camp," Ries ordered.

"Watch me," I replied. "I'm the ruling Prince, you said so yourself, which means I'm the one that makes the decisions."

Ries and Troy both looked at me with a mixture of emotions but didn't respond. They knew I was right. I had the final decision-making power and I intended to use it in this case. They were also excited that I started to accept my destiny.

"I'm going to get changed," I said again. "Gather up the troops that you want to take with us because we're going to save Aerian and we're leaving in ten minutes."

I entered my designated tent in the center of the camp and immediately saw Oaren lying on a blanket on the ground. A small oil lamp illuminated the space. Oaren stared at me. I didn't know he was sharing the tent with me,

"I came to get changed," I told him. "Then I'm going."

"This is your tent too," he said sharply.

"I know," I replied almost as sharply, "but Aerian is in trouble and I made the decision to go save her tonight."

"Don't you think we should rest and train first?"

"No. She is being tortured. I saw a vision when I was washing off in the river. The Knights had her chained and they were hitting her. They were looking for something. The Knight said 'Bazo telos se. Opou einai o orasi'."

Oaren sat up quickly and then climbed to his feet. "Did you say 'orasi'?"

"Yes."

"They're looking for it."

"What? What are they looking for? What do they mean by 'sight'?"

"I'm going out of the tent so you can get changed in private. Hurry."

Oaren left the tent and I immediately slid my wet boxers off and then took a new pair out of the bag from the tailor and put them on. I wrapped a blue tunic around my waist and put the top piece on. Similar to the one I first wore from the store, the top was too short for my expectations. I figured it was better to have some covering over my upper body than none at all.

I took the second pair of boots out of the bag and put them on. My belt, sword, and a scabbard sat on the ground near the entrance to the tent. I hooked the belt around my waist, the scabbard to the belt, and then slid my sword into place. I fixed my necklace and made sure it was holding up. Then I grabbed the map that lay near the blanket and headed out of the tent. I folded the map up and slid it into my waistline.

"My Prince," Troy said when I joined him, Ries, and Oaren outside the tent, "you do know that going into the city at night is asking for trouble?"

"Why? What's so bad about the city at night?"

"Well the city is said to be nykterinos," Troy said. "Or in English, nocturnal".

"What does that mean?" I questioned.

Oaren, Ries, and Troy looked at each other. Ries answered, "It means that there are things that happen in the city at night that are not very pleasant. Criminal activity is high at night. Robberies, murders, and illegal magic are high after dark. Most people that live in the city do not go out after dark." Ries stopped talking to check my expression.

"As I told you before," Oaren picked up, "you do not know Atlantis yet. In fact, there are many parts that you do not want to know. Atlantis can be a very dangerous place. It is not the mythical fantasy world that your culture reads about. We have the same issues your cities deal with, except we also have dark magic. It is illegal to practice dark magic in Atlantis but it still happens."

"And I would guess that the Knights are trying to convince the magicians that practice dark magic to join with them," said Ries. "They can promise to make it legal under their rule."

"Lucky for us," I said, "it's probably going to take us 'til daylight to get to the city."

"We do not want to attack by day," Ries informed me.

"But you don't want to go at night," I reminded him.

"I did not say I did not want to go at night. I was just telling you what we are getting ourselves into. I would prefer to rest tonight and train you in the morning and for a few days before going into battle with the Knights. But you are the ruling Prince. If you say we attack tonight, we attack tonight. My only suggestion is that we go by aftokinero so it is still dark when we approach the city."

"Do we have enough aftokineros?" Oaren asked.

"We cannot take our entire group," Ries said. "We need to go

in a small group. This is a covert operation." I almost commended him on his knowledge of the English language but then I remembered he was speaking in Atlantean and my brain was automatically translating. I figured I should commend myself instead.

"We can take my family's..." Oaren started and then stopped. "I mean we can take *my* Aftokinero."

"And I have one that I parked nearby," Troy told us.

"Who will be going?" I asked.

"You will go with Oaren in his aftokinero," said Ries. "I will ride with you two in case something goes wrong. Troy can take his aftokinero and we will send his brother and another soldier with him. That will be enough."

"Do we have a plan for how we get into the palace?" asked Troy.

"We will have to set the aftokineros down on the outskirts of the city," answered Ries. "We can work out how to get to the palace and invade once we get into the city." That didn't make me feel confident. I would've liked to have a distinct plan for invasion. But it was settled, we were going to rescue Aerian.

"I will get my brother and another soldier," Troy said. "We will meet you on the West banks of the city, right at the main fishing dock."

"That sounds good," Ries said.

Troy started to walk away but Ries yelled, "stamato". Troy stopped and turned and waited for Ries to continue. Ries made sure he had eye contact and then continued, "We all want to save the sorceress but realize that our first priority is to keep the Prince safe. Everyone on this mission must assure me that they will honor the oath to protect our ruler, no matter what."

I looked at Troy and then Oaren; they were both nodding and they verbally agreed to protect me with their lives.

"And you, Trey," Ries said. "You must accept your position as ruling Prince. If we do this, we have to know that you will follow through. We cannot do this and then have you leave us without a leader."

I stared at him, uncomfortable with what he was saying. His eyes met mine and that made me even more uncomfortable. It sunk in; there was no turning back. We were going to set into motion a revolution that could either save Atlantis or leave it destroyed in the process. And there was no arguing it, I had to accept my place as ruling Prince and I had to take responsibility for whatever the outcome was.

I took a deep breath, pushed my stomach back into its proper place and then said, "I accept my position as ruling Prince. I take the oath to lead Atlantis with its best interests in mind and I accept responsibility for the consequences of my decisions and actions."

Troy, Oaren, and Ries smiled at me and then Troy left to find his brother and another soldier. Without another word, Ries and Oaren signaled for me to follow them. Taking another breath, I followed them, now carrying the weight of an entire island on my shoulders.

I sat in Oaren's aftokinero, the air around me much cooler on the river. I remembered how much fun it was the first time I was in the aftokinero, as Oaren took me into the city. Anxiety hit me. Not only were we about to race on water clouds toward the city in the middle of the night, but we were also heading straight into a fight.

Ries sat directly behind me and, even though I couldn't see him, I could tell that he was watching the environment around us with vigilance. Every second I spent with Ries gave me a reason to trust him a little more. I realized he wanted to defeat the Knights and that he wanted to ensure my safety so I could rule the island.

Oaren dipped his left hand in the water and then ran it over the steering wheel. The car spoke "Poios einai odigisi?".

Oaren looked at me, as if he wanted me to stop him from taking the next step. I didn't say anything. I couldn't tell him not to take us; we had to save Aerian.

"Poios einai odigisi?" asked the car again.

Oaren took a deep breath and said, "Afto einai Oaren".

The shot of electricity tore through the night. After the water started flowing through the car, it went quiet again. I still couldn't believe how the car could pull water in and shoot it out without making a sound or me feeling the vibration.

"Ochi strofi piso," Oaren said in a voice laced with fear. He pulled down on the lever next to the wheel and the car sucked in the water and pushed it out in a giant wave. Less than a second later, we shot straight into the air, water forced toward the ground below us. We landed in a synnero, Oaren moved the lever to the middle position, and the car raced forward.

I sat back and closed my eyes as the cool wind whipped at me. My stomach lurched as Oaren took a sharp turn and connected with another synnero. Opening my eyes, I realized it was very difficult to see anything in the dark. The aftokinero did not have any lights on it. I looked at Oaren and I could tell he was following the path in his mind; he was driving on instinct alone.

Ries leaned forward and yelled over the wind, "remember to set us down at the main dock on the Western edge."

Oaren nodded his head but remained focused on trying to stay with the synnero.

"It's a really good thing that there are not many aftokineros around at night," I said. Oaren didn't respond. I stared at the city that was now in front of us. In the center of that city sat a palace. My palace. Not only did I want to save Aerian from the dungeon where she was held captive but I also wanted to run the Knights out of my palace. Now that I'd accepted my destiny, I had to make sure I fulfilled it. And that meant defeating the Knights.

"Approaching drop zone," Oaren said. "Hang on." He pushed the lever up and the aftokinero slowed. With the final push of the lever, the car dropped out of the sky and into the river below.

The aftokinero settled on the river and then I climbed out. Oaren tied the aftokinero to a dock post while Ries scoped out the area. The city was quiet, eerily so, and most buildings were completely dark. Tall structures that reminded me of the streetlights in Miami had flames burning at the top that provided a dim light to the area around the docks.

Three shadows walked toward us and Ries placed his hand on his sword. They stepped into the light of a lamp, Troy was leading the trio, his brother and another soldier behind him. Troy and his brother could have passed for twins. The other soldier, a large, muscled man with dark hair and a scruffy face, didn't fit the Atlantean image I had put together since being on the island. But I was glad to have someone of his size protecting me.

"How do we get to the palace?" Troy asked Ries when we all gathered in a group.

"There are two options," Ries informed us. "We can go on foot, which is rather dangerous since it is more likely that we will be noticed while walking around the city this time of night. The other is by river. The river that runs just south of here actually flows from the northern part of the island, right under the palace, and into the Atlantic Ocean on the southwestern side of the island. Problem is, we will have to swim against the current."

Everyone looked at me, as though I was supposed to make the decision. "I might be the Prince now," I said, "but I'm not a soldier and I don't know anything about planning an attack. You're the experts."

Ries thought for a moment and then said, "if we go by river, we can get into the dungeon part of the palace easier than on land. I am sure we will still encounter some Knights but I think it is a better option to go by river."

"I agree," Troy said. His brother and the other soldier nodded.

"We have to walk just a little south to the river," Ries told us. "Keep careful watch." He looked at me with sincerity. "Stay in the center of our group."

I nodded to show him that I understood and then we started our trek to the river. "Why can't we just hop in the river we landed in?"

"Because it runs in a loop around the city," Ries told me. "We could swim our way to the river but there is no point. It is not a far walk and then we do not have to swim as far."

A few minutes later, we stood on the bank of the river that seemed to cross the moat that circled the city. The current was quick and I knew it would be difficult to swim against it. The buildings, like at the docks, were dark and the streets quiet. Upstream, the river cut through buildings, creating a street of water. Bridges stretched across to connect the two banks.

"Everyone ready?" Ries asked.

"Are you going to be able to swim in this current?" Troy asked me with concern.

"I'm a champion swimmer," I told him. "I'll do just fine."

"If we swim upstream, we will eventually come to the wall that protects the royal grounds," Ries explained. "It is about four miles from here. At that point, we will probably encounter the Knights as I expect them to be guarding the wall and moat just inside the wall. However, I think there are gates that we can pull out in order to get under the wall and into the royal grounds. Once inside the royal grounds, if we follow the river, we will end up in the basement of the palace. As I said before, the river runs right under the palace and the palace basement was built to incorporate the use of the river for the royals.

"That is where I will no longer know how to lead us to Aerian. I do not know where she is being held captive." He looked at me, hoping for the answer.

His stare, and my desire to find her, jogged my memory of one of the connections I had with Aerian. The one I had in the river just before the attack at Oaren's house seemed to provide the answers.

I listened to Aerian's voice in my head. *Main River. Fourth grate on the left. Three floors down. Second door on the left.*

"I know how to find her once we're in the palace grounds," I announced. "Aerian gave me directions during one of our connections."

Ries nodded and then turned his attention to the river. "Follow me." He jumped into the river and started swimming against the current. Oaren and I jumped at the same time and then Troy and the two other soldiers followed immediately after us.

After what felt like hours of swimming in the cold river, Oaren asked for a break and I couldn't have been happier to support him. Ries wasn't excited about taking a break but we couldn't just keep swimming with our arms and legs in so much pain.

"We can break for a few minutes," Ries shouted to us. We swam to the right bank of the river and climbed out. I lay on the rocky shore, breathing profusely, and wished for my throbbing muscles to relax. The sky above me was cloudless, with the exception of the synneros. Miami felt as far away as the bright stars that broke the dark blanket.

"How far did we swim?" Oaren asked. He lay next to me, staring at the sky.

"We are three quarters of the way to the royal grounds," Ries answered. I could tell, by the way Ries' voice met my ears, he was standing up.

"It feels like we swam for hours," replied Oaren.

"We did," said Ries. "We were swimming for over two hours already. But we do not have much time to make it to the palace in the cover of darkness; dawn is just a couple hours away. With how tired we are, we have at least another hour ahead of us."

"Ugh," I cried. "I don't think I can swim for another hour in these currents. I probably swallowed half of the river already."

No one responded to me but feet shuffled away. I lifted my head to see what was going on. Ries, Troy, and the two other soldiers were huddled in a little group. I wanted to know what they were talking about but, too tired to move, I rested my head on the ground again.

"I am with you," Oaren said out of nowhere. "I cannot swim anymore."

"I'm a champion swimmer but I can't handle swimming this far with the current against us. I could easily do it without the current."

"Maybe we could walk for a while and then get back in the river when we get closer to the royal grounds."

I turned my head to face him. "That's not a bad idea but I'm not sure it's safe."

Oaren sighed. "It is not safe to be swimming when we are this tired. We might drown."

A new voice cracked the night air. "Stratiotis!"

More yelling from the area around us forced me to sit up and Oaren did the same.

Ries turned to me, then back to his soldiers. "Stoteinos magos."

"Dark magicians?" I translated.

"I think it is time to run," Oaren said. We climbed to our feet at the same time.

"Oaren," Troy yelled, "take our Prince and run for the royal grounds. Go!"

"You heard him," Oaren pushed me to run.

Purple light exploded in front of us and we were pushed backwards by a hot wind. A green swirl wrapped around my feet, I lost my balance, and collapsed on the hard ground.

"Trey," Oaren called. A red vine of mist wrapped around his body and seemed to paralyze him. He fell flat, face first, to the ground.

I climbed to my feet and looked for the soldiers. Ries was in

battle with a magician in dark robes. Troy and his brother were cooperatively fighting another magician, using their swords to thwart spells, at least as much as possible. I didn't see the other soldier; the big, quiet one.

"Trey, run!" Oaren yelled, still wrapped in red fog. I listened to him, to some degree anyway, but instead of running toward the royal grounds, I went to him and started pulling at the mist. As I ripped the fog off of him, it dissipated into the dark night. Once I freed his arms, he fought to break out of the vine around the rest of his body.

"Now we run," I told him. He climbed to his feet and led me away from the scene.

"Check the map," said Oaren. "It will tell us if anyone else who means us harm is around."

"It's soaking wet," I replied.

"It does not matter; the map is magic and will still work."

The map revealed dozens of buildings around us, all the way to the royal grounds. Unfortunately, the map was scattered with glowing red dots.

"Do you think there are that many dark magicians?" I asked.

"No," Oaren answered. "Remember, we are getting closer to

the palace, which means the Knights have a higher presence." I didn't

feel any better that the red dots were Knights; either way we weren't safe.

"I think we need to swim again." Oaren veered toward the river.

"Not..." The Knights came around a corner in front of us. "I couldn't agree more." I followed him into the river, hugged the bank, and moved as quietly as possible. The Knights' voices faded as they walked past and we started swimming upstream again.

A flash of blue wrapped around us. The water went still and grew cold against my skin. I searched for a cause. On the bank, a magician chanted a spell and waved a wand. A chunk of ice floated past me.

"He's turning the river to ice," Oaren cried. "We have to climb out before it's too late."

The water burned my skin with cold. I climbed onto the shore and Oaren followed. The magician stopped chanting and turned toward the Knights that had walked past us just a few minutes before.

"He's going to call the Knights back," said Oaren.

Pulling my sword out of its scabbard, I ran toward the magician and prepared to strike. The old man turned around and waved his wand at me. I flew backwards and crashed to the ground. Oaren ran past me toward the man. The wand moved up over the man's head and Oaren's body followed, flipped over the man, and smacked into the ground.

The magician yelled for the Knights as I climbed to my feet. The Knights stepped in line with the sorcerer as I took a defensive stance. The old man held his wand tight and laughed. "You think you stand a chance against us, boy? The Knights of the Abyss have aligned with dark magic and are unstoppable. Those of us that have been suppressed for thousands of years are free to practice as we wish."

"Not if I can help it," I told him. I moved toward him but before I could even take three steps, he slashed his wand like a knife cutting into butter. Something tore at the flesh of my chest. I screamed in pain and moved my hand to the wound; warm liquid covered my hand in great quantities. Too weak to stand, I collapsed and prepared to die.

Oaren jumped on the old man from behind, the force great enough to knock him to the ground, sending his wand sliding across the gravel toward me. I reached for the wand with the little strength I had left but one of the Knights kicked it away from me before I could grasp it. Seconds later, I felt a sword tip on my throat.

"Stamato," yelled Ries as he ran from an alley with Troy and his brother. It was not a good sign that the other soldier was still missing. The brothers went directly for the Knights and the magician while Ries ran toward me. The sword tip moved away from my throat and I heard metal clang with metal as the world faded away.

Eischoro

Light flooded into my eyes. I immediately searched for the battle that took place as I passed out. I didn't see anyone or hear any metal clanging. Just bright light. I searched for the source and found sunshine coming through an open window near my head. The warm room was a nice change from the icy river I had escaped. The smell of freshly baked bread, reminded me of my hunger.

"How do you feel?" Oaren asked me as he entered the room.

"Like I was hit by a truck."

"By a what?"

"Never mind. What happened?"

"You passed out from loss of blood after the magician slashed you with some type of magic."

"How long was I out?"

"About ten hours." I tried to move but Oaren reprimanded me, "you need to rest. You are not fully healed yet."

I looked at the bedroom around me, which was very similar to the one I stayed in at Oaren's house. "Where are we?"

"Ries and the other two soldiers killed the Knights and the magician and then they quickly moved us to this house. I think the man that owns this house is a retired military general."

"And obviously it's daytime," I said. "I suppose our mission was postponed?"

"For now," Oaren said. "Ries, Troy, and Broden are meeting with the general."

"Broden?"

"Troy's brother. I finally learned his name."

"What about the other soldier?"

"We do not know what happened to him. We assume he was killed but we did not find a body."

"And you?"

Oaren looked at me, his expression turning to hurt. He sat down in an old rocking chair next to the bed. "I am holding up as well as can be expected. I do not blame you anymore. Ries talked to me and helped me realize that the Knights are to blame for what happened. He also told me that the only way we are going to set this right is to accept you as our Prince and help you take control of the island. My Mom and Dad wanted you to lead us and I do not want them to have died in vain."

"Me neither. I'm glad that we can be friends again. I feel bad about what happened but I didn't cause it."

"I accept that." Oaren looked toward the door of the bed-room. "Do you want some freshly baked bread? It is very good."

"I'd love some. I'm starving." I went to climb out of bed but the pain was too great to move.

"Stay put, I will bring some bread to you." Oaren left the room and I closed my eyes.

The plan changed. We didn't make it to save Aerian last night so I wanted to talk about another plan. But I needed to get past this pain first.

Oaren returned with bread and a glass of water on a tray. Ries, Troy, Broden and a man with white hair came in shortly after him. I started devouring the bread as soon as Oaren handed me the tray. I never found plain bread appetizing but this was delicious. A

sweet dough, full of flavor.

"It is an honor to host you in my home, my Prince," the old man said. His wrinkled face had a long scar on the right cheek.

"Thank you for allowing us to rest and for the bread," I re-plied.

Ries spoke with a purpose. "While you were sleeping, we talked about gathering support for you. Kamau is a retired soldier and he has many friends who are also retired soldiers. He is going to call and get their help in gathering troops for you. They know many active soldiers that he feels they will be able to convince to side with us and help us defeat the Knights."

"That's great," I said through the chewing.

"The Knights we encountered last night are dead," Ries continued. "So is the magician. But we have to assume that others know that we are in the city. Kamau is taking a chance by allowing us to rest in his home."

"Nonsense," Kamau said. "The Prince must recuperate."

"The spell is wearing off quickly as his body regains strength," said Ries, as though I wasn't in the room. "He will be ready to leave by nightfall."

I wasn't so sure but I didn't have a choice. Not only did we need to keep from being discovered but I also wanted to rescue Aerian as soon as possible. I looked at my chest, which, as Ries indicated, was healing rather quickly.

"So I assume that the dark magicians have aligned with the Knights of the Abyss?" I questioned.

"That is how it appears," Ries said. "But that will not be a problem once Kamau and his friends gather troops and we rescue Aerian. Being a true sorceress, she is much more powerful than those who practice dark magic."

"Anyone can learn to cast spells," Oaren told me, "but if it is in your blood, that is a different story altogether. Magic is in Aerian's blood. Real, ancient magic.

"We best let the Prince rest," Kamau said. "We can continue our plan for gaining support in the kitchen while I bake some more bread, since the Prince seemed to enjoy it."

"It was delicious," I told him. "Thank you."

"Rest up," Ries said. "We must leave at nightfall." Everyone left and they closed the bedroom door behind them. I closed my eyes and drifted back into unconsciousness.

Oaren woke me up by shaking my arm and calling my name. I oriented myself and then sat up, still sore where the dark magic had cut me. All that remained of the gash was a faint, red line.

Everyone had gathered in the room to see how I was doing. Four candles provided a glow to the room. The world outside the window was dim with nightfall. Ries' eyes told me we had to get moving.

"Here, my Prince," Kamau said, "please eat before you leave." He placed a tray with bread, cheese, and a few shrimp on my lap. Not my first choice in meals but I was hungry again so I graciously accepted.

Ries picked my sword up, as well as the map, and laid it on a dresser so that it was ready for me when I was done eating. Then he turned and said, "Kamau will work to gather troops while we penetrate the palace to find Aerian. Once we save Aerian, we are going directly to the hidden fortress of the Atlantean military. Kamau and his friends are going to do their best to get as many soldiers as possible to meet us there."

I took another bite of bread and looked at him with concern.

"We are going to battle the Knights," Ries said.

I swallowed the bread. "I'm not sure we're ready to engage in a battle."

"We will not have a choice," Ries told me. "Once we enter that palace and rescue Aerian, they will wage war on us. We must be ready to fight back. If Kamau and his friends can gather enough soldiers then all we will need is a plan of attack."

"Attack?" I asked. "I thought you were talking about defense."

"We need to take back this island," Ries said. "You are the rul-ing Prince, as you accepted, and you must have your palace and a chance to reorganize our government. You cannot do that while the Knights are in the palace. Besides, it is a disgrace to our people and our history to have such an evil group on the royal grounds."

I was only sixteen and they wanted me to reorganize their government. I didn't even fully understand the government I grew up in and now I was supposed to lead one that I knew nothing about.

Kamau looked at me with empathy; he knew why I felt the way I did. "My Prince," he said, "this is your home now. You have Atlantis in your blood. You must accept that and you must fight for this island as though your life depends on it, because it does. The people want to rebel but they need a leader. You can be that

leader and you can find your true destiny in the process."

Ries was not as caring. The look on his face told me to suck it up and deal with it because they needed me to be the prince.

I finished the shrimp, bread, and a piece of cheese. Oaren handed me a glass of water and I drank it quickly. I stood up and fixed my tunic and then placed the sword in the scabbard and the map in my waistline.

"Good luck," Kamau said. "I hope to see all of you soon."

"Thank you," Ries said.

"Thank you," I joined in. "I really appreciate your hospitality." Kamau nodded and led us to the front door.

"We are just a few blocks from the royal grounds," Ries told us. "The Knights now know that we are in the city so I expect that their vigilance has increased. Be ready for their attack at all times. Our goal is to walk as close to the wall as possible and then use the river to get under the walls and into the palace. That plan did not change."

"This is a suicide mission," Oaren said. We all looked at him, his face filled with fear. "We are not going to survive this. We should gather the soldiers and then attack. This is not a good idea."

"You can stay here if you choose," Ries told him. "We are go-ing to make our move because it will start the war."

I looked at Oaren and supported Ries. "We have to save Aerian. She'll be able to help us against the Knights. Like Ries said, you are welcome to stay here."

Without another word, Ries opened the door and walked out in the dark. Troy and Broden followed him and I followed them. Before we even took ten steps away from the house, Oaren ran after us.

It didn't take us long to reach the wall of the royal grounds and, to our surprise, we didn't encounter any Knights along the way. We stood in an alley and observed the wall. There was movement on top, definitely Knights keeping watch.

"We need a way to distract the Knights," Ries said. He looked at Troy and Broden. "Can you two divert their attention so that Oaren, Trey, and I can get into the river and try to gain access?"

They looked at each other and smiled; I could tell that they loved the idea. They seemed like the type of brothers that loved to work together to cause problems so this was right up their alley. "We can definitely do that," Troy said.

"Get to it," Ries said. The brothers ran out into the open in front of the wall and started screaming and shouting. "I hope they do not get themselves killed." Ries took us back through the alley and we connected with a passageway between two houses. He led us out on to the main street and then jumped into the river. Oaren and I followed, reluctantly, and we swam close to the bank all the way to an underwater grate at the base of the wall.

Ries called us over and then signaled for us to remain quiet. "Just inside the wall there is a moat, a circle of water that runs all the way around the royal grounds. There is a port for ships where this river meets the moat. Once we get inside, we must stay submerged as much as possible to avoid being seen. When you do come up for air, make sure it is close to the bank to conceal yourself as much as possible.

"When we get inside, we are going to swim to the left, which, if we follow the moat, will reconnect with this river on the other side of the palace. At that point, the current will be to our advantage and we can make our way into the basement of the palace."

Screaming interrupted Ries' plan and an alarm sounded from inside the wall. "They are attending to Troy and Broden," said Ries, "this is our chance." He dove under and pulled at the rusted grate. Ries tore the grate right out and laid it on the bottom of the river. I made myself a mental note to fix all river grates in and out of the city and royal grounds once I had control of the island as I followed Ries under the wall.

We took a breath and rested against the bank and then turned left into the moat, dove down, and swam as far as we could until we had to get more air. I took the time to admire the palace from a distance. It was impressive, even in the dark. Lights from burning candles shimmered in the windows. The massive building's architecture and design were stunning by moonlight.

"Keep moving," Ries whispered. An arrow struck the water and a man on the wall yelled. "We were spotted." Ries climbed out of the river as quickly as he could. "Keep going," he told us and then ran toward the wall.

Another alarm sounded, this time signaling that intruders had breached the wall. Oaren and I swam as fast as we could. I dove under and my necklace lit up quickly, the light shining intensely on the underground bank of the river to my right.

Are you in, my Prince? Aerian connected with me.

In the moat outside the palace. I informed her.

Use one of the secret tunnels in the bank of the moat.

Oaren swam ahead of me but I called him back the best I could under water. I pointed at the wall of the river where the light was focused. I brushed my hand against the bank but my arm went through it, into an empty space.

"It's an illusion," I said to Oaren, though he probably couldn't understand me under water. We swam through what looked like dirt and ended up leaving the river and entering a dry tunnel of stone blocks.

"Spells can do some pretty cool things," I said.

"Now what?" asked Oaren.

"We follow this tunnel and see where it leads us."

"You do not know where it leads us?"

"Aerian told me about it in a vision I had just a minute ago. The one thing I'm fairly certain about is that the Knights don't know about this tunnel. My guess is only the royals and their sorcerers know about it."

"Well we can hope for that," Oaren said as he looked around. "After all, the rest of our group is already battling with the Knights so I hope we do not get separated."

"Let's go," I ignored his comment and led him quickly through the dark tunnel. I hoped that we would find our way to the main river that flows under the palace because then I could use the directions Aerian gave me to find her.

The tunnel forked into two passageways. The sound of the river came from the left tunnel so I chose that one and increased my pace. Oaren followed me into the river and the current carried us to the edge of the palace. A grate stopped us from flowing out from under the building. I found it ironic that the grate was supposed to keep things out of the palace but instead it was keeping us in.

I dove under and waited until my necklace lit up. *Aerian.* I searched for the connection.

Are you in the palace?

Yes. I'm going to follow your directions. We'll be there soon.

Use the map. The Knights know you are here. You must be careful.

I surfaced and looked at Oaren. "Aerian says that the Knights know that we are here." I pulled the map out of my tunic and stared at it. There were no red dots on the entire level of the place. "We're clear, for now."

"Where do we go?"

I tucked the map back in, "Fourth grate on the left. Three floors down. Second door on the left."

Sozo Kai Drapetero

I pulled the grate out from the wall and entered a hallway similar to the secret one we used to gain access to the palace.

"This is incredible," Oaren exclaimed. "All of the stories of the underground passages are true. I wonder if they really do run under the entire island."

"That's something for you to explore once we move into the palace," I told him.

He looked at me with awe, "I can move into the palace too?"

"Of course. You're part of this battle so you deserve the re-ward." His face showed pure joy. It seemed like that was the best thing he'd ever heard.

The hallway ended with stairs leading up and down. Lantern flames flickered on the walls of the stairs, which curved as they ascended or descended.. "Three floors down," I said out loud.

I pulled the map out and studied it carefully was we made our way down, past one floor and then another with no signs of red dots. Red dots appeared on the map as we approached the level we needed to enter. At least a dozen of them darkened when we stood just outside the main hallway.

"Aha," I said, "that makes sense. All of the Knights are near Aerian."

"That does make sense," Oaren agreed.

I studied the map. "There are three Knights in the hallway. We have to take them out first."

"Take them out?"

Oaren's mastery of the English language made me forget that it was not native to him. "Put them out of action," I clarified. "Either knock them out or kill them. Preferably the former, I don't want to kill any more than I already did."

"But they will kill us," said Oaren. "They already killed my parents."

"But that doesn't mean we have to stoop to their level." I waited to see if he wanted to respond but he didn't. "There are four inside the room next to where Aerian indicated she was being held captive and there are five in the room with her. After we take care of the three in the hallway, we should first attend to the Knights in the room next to Aerian so that we don't get ambushed once we find Aerian."

"Sounds like a solid plan to me."

I smiled but prevented a laugh. Two teenage boys deciding if a plan of attack was solid or not wasn't assuring to me. What did we know about battles?

"After we rescue Aerian, I'm not sure what to do. Ries said we could go to the secret soldier base but I don't know where that is; maybe Aerian does." I looked at him and hoped he would save the day by saying that he knew where the base was but of course he didn't. "Ready?" I pulled my sword from the scabbard.

"You do realize that Ries never gave me a sword?"

Truth was, I hadn't realized that. That was a problem. "I'll take out the first Knight, you take his sword." Not a great plan but we didn't have any other choice. "Here we go!"

I ran down the hall as fast as I could and sliced at the first Knight I encountered. He blocked my sword with his and the metal clang echoed off the stone blocks. The other Knights turned their attention to our fight and came to support their friend. Three Knights surrounded and swung their swords at me. I blocked each one with my weapon and forced them away for a few seconds, just enough to stop the next one from dealing a fatal blow.

One Knight aimed the tip of his blade right at my forehead, I ducked as he struck. He tried to redirect the blade but still missed me and instead pierced the Knight that was behind me in the chest. I took advantage of the moment of shock and quickly stabbed the third Knight in the chest and removed my sword. The Knight collapsed as the other one pulled his blade from his comrade's chest and turned his focus to me. He swung his sword at me but I blocked it and, before he could take another swipe, Oaren stabbed him with a sword he took from a dead Knight.

"Three down," I said, "nine to go. Let's hit the first room on the left; Aerian is in the second."

Before I could even finish my sentence, four Knights from the first room came into the hallway, looking for the Knights that were now dead. They saw us, yelled for backup, and one ran down the hallway toward the stairs.

"He is going to get reinforcements," Oaren cried.

I met swords with one of the remaining three Knights and pushed him away. Another attacked me from behind but I was able to spin in enough time to catch his blade. Oaren fought the third Knight who quickly overpowered and knocked him to the ground.

Adrenaline flooded my veins. I stabbed the Knight that tried to attack me from behind in the stomach. I turned and hit the other one as hard as I could in the head with the seahorse handle of my sword and he fell to the ground unconscious. The remaining Knight stood over Oaren, his sword tip aiming at his heart. I attacked unexpectedly and knocked him out in the same manner I did the other.

"Drag the two unconscious ones into the room," I told Oaren. We quickly pulled them into the room and closed the door.

"What are you doing?" he asked. "We still have five more to battle."

"Their outfits are perfectly fine, we didn't cut them in anyway."

"You want to..."

"Exactly. We're going to take their clothes and pass ourselves off as Knights."

Stripping the clothes off a man was something I never expected to do and something I hoped I never had to do again. We dressed as quickly as we could and finished by wrapping the headpiece around our heads and covering our faces, save for our eyes. I looked at the two men lying on the floor. Without the Knights' ninja-like outfits, the two individuals looked like normal Atlanteans. I knew then that if I hoped to put an end to the Knights of the Abyss, I would have to discover what caused normal Atlanteans to turn on their government.

"Now we save Aerian," I told Oaren as I hooked my sword in the scabbard and tucked the map into my pants. "You have the Atlantean accent that I don't have so you should do all of the talking. Just make sure to use a deep voice."

"Got it," Oaren practiced a coarse voice.

"Perfect." I opened the door and we walked to the next room, which was still shut.

Six Knights entered the hallway from the stairs. One of them mumbled something about the intruders in Atlantean and Oaren replied by telling them that they ran down the hall. The six Knights ran in the direction Oaren told them and I opened the door to the room Aerian indicated.

The room looked like it did in the mind connections, only now I could see more of the room and it reminded me of a police station with one jail cell. The five Knights stood in front of the cell, swords drawn and ready to attack. Aerian's bruised body barely stood chained to the wall.

One of the Knights asked us what we were doing. Oaren answered, in a perfect Knight voice, "Emeis blepe be apeiloumenos kai emeis blepe be anagki eis tis synodos." I quickly translated Oaren's statement in my mind. *We are under threat and we need to escort her.*

"Under the orders of whom?" one of the Knights questioned.

I knew Oaren was stumped. How was he supposed to know who would give those orders?

"Emeis blepe be anagki eis tis synodos," Oaren told them again, as though repeating the orders again would convince them to let us take her out of the room.

The Knights inspected us carefully and started speaking in a language I could not interpret. Oaren moved his head closer to mine. "Ancient Egyptian. I do not speak Ancient Egyptian."

A Knight stepped forward and walked a circle around us, his sword ready to strike. He stepped back in line with the others and signaled for them to open the cell. Two Knights opened the cell, unchained Aerian, and carried her to us. Oaren and I each took one of her arms and supported her so she wouldn't collapse.

I nodded at the Knights and then Oaren and I carefully turned and started toward the door with Aerian between us.

"Tou spathi!" a Knight yelled from behind us. "Tou spathi!"

"They noticed your sword," Oaren cried. I grabbed the sea-horse handle of my sword; it was a dead giveaway that I wasn't a Knight.

"Run," I cried. We moved as quickly as we could, dragging Aerian with us. We only ran for a few seconds before the Knights caught up and we had to let go of Aerian and fend off their sword strikes.

Aerian rested against the wall, standing, which surprised me. Oaren and I fought the swords of the five Knights. I ripped off my headpiece; I figured if we were discovered I might as well be able to see and breathe a little easier. A sword nearly clipped my face but I dodged it and sliced back, missing its handler.

Flames burned past my eyes and engulfed the five Knights, leaving them screaming in agony. Oaren and I backed away from the heat and then turned to find Aerian standing and smiling at her handy work.

"How did you do that?" Oaren questioned.

"Explanations later, we need to get out of the palace." Acrian ran toward the stairs and we followed.

"We have soldiers meeting us in the secret military base," I said as I ran after her. "Do you know where that is?"

"Of course," she said. "The only people that know about that are the royals, their sorcerers, and the soldiers directly responsible for protecting them."

"Can we get there quickly?"

Aerian led us down the stairs we had used to invade. "There is an underground river and cavern system that runs the entire island. It is legend to the people of Atlantis but is studied carefully by the royals as escape routes."

"If my friends could see me now!" Oaren exclaimed.

We descended what appeared to be three more floors and then Aerian stopped us at a dead-end wall. She turned to face us. "No doubt the Knights have been down here but they would have no idea how to access the caverns. She tapped five blocks, in what I assumed was a pattern of about twenty strikes, and a chunk of the wall separated from the rest and slid to the left, revealing an opening to a cave. We entered the cave and Aerian closed the wall behind us.

Hippocampus Syndesi

Aerian found an ancient torch by the entrance to the cave and lit it—not on fire—on magic. She led us deep into the cavern system and, even though I had thousands of questions in my head, I was too busy observing the incredible world around me to ask them. Streams ran through the cave and stalactites and stalagmites—I couldn't remember which was which—grew from the ceiling and floor. Ponds of water created beautiful pools of refreshingly cool liquid to drink. I even thought I saw a bat, which completed my preconceived vision of caves.

I was reminded of the cavern I saw in the vision when Jocasta and the Knight attacked me but I figured the chances were slim that we would run into them now. We walked for a long time, probably close to an hour, saying very little with the exception of

commenting on the beauty around us.

Finally, Aerian stopped and said, "we should rest. We are now in the safest place on the island." I thought about Ries, Troy and Broden on the surface above us. I wondered if they were still battling the Knights and trying to find us.

Aerian sat down on a large rock and rubbed her shoulders and arms, which must have been sore from hanging for days. "So why didn't you just battle your way out of captivity?" I asked her.

"What do you mean?" she asked. Her dark eyes focused on me. Her skin was near pale; her hair the color of the cave rocks around me, yet there was something very attractive about her.

"You had enough magic to burn the Knights when we rescued you but yet you allowed them to hold you hostage. Why?"

"Dark magicians put a spell on the cell I was in," she explained. "While in the cell, my magic was useless but, once you took me away from the cell, my power returned."

"If you couldn't access your magic while you were in the cell, why could we communicate through our minds?"

She smiled and hid a little laugh. "That is not magic, my Prince. There is something greater involved with the mental connections."

"What?"

"My Prince, you have a lot to learn about Atlantis and her people. You are going to lead us into a new era and if you want to do that successfully, you must take the time to understand the history and culture of our island."

"Someone has to teach me." I sat down on a rock across from Aerian. "I've been asking questions and trying to learn but no one wanted to teach me."

"I will teach you. But first we should rest."

"I'm not tired," I said.

"I am exhausted and it appears that Oaren is all worn out." Oaren was asleep on the cave floor.

"Can I ask one question before you sleep?"

"Of course," she settled herself onto the floor near Oaren.

"Why me? Why do I have the necklace that makes me the Prince? Why did you call on me to save you?"

"That was actually three questions," she corrected me with a beautiful smile. "They are very elaborate and will take a very long time to answer." She paused. "I promise that I will answer them in due time. For now, I will say that there is something very special about you. You are the one predicted in the prophecy. I am not sure what that means but in due time it will be revealed." She closed her eyes.

The one predicted in the prophecy. In due time it will be revealed. That sounded like what Grandpa told me before I found out he wasn't really my grandfather. Her answer didn't help at all. In fact it gave me even more questions. How did she know I was special? And what was special about me? Was it the same thing Kristjana saw in me? And what did the prophecy mean for me?

I got up and stepped away from where Oaren and Aerian slept and found myself at the edge of a pond. I looked deep into the water, at my reflection in a mirror. I looked for something special in myself. I figured that I couldn't see whatever qualities I had that made me unique because they were part of me. It took an outsider to discover those qualities and point them out to me.

I lay down on the ground next to the pond and stared at the ceiling of the cave. I had accomplished the first major part of my mission. Aerian was safe. But I still wanted answers. What was this prophecy Aerian talked about? Who were my real parents? How was I supposed to save Atlantis? Technically, I could leave all of that alone and go home and try to get my life back in order. But I couldn't leave Aerian, Oaren, Ries, Troy, and Broden to deal with the Knights of the Abyss. Whether I liked it or not, I was connected to each of them and I wouldn't feel right leaving them on an island of turmoil. No one could predict what the Knights would do next.

I didn't think I was tired when I had the opportunity to ask Aerian the questions but now that I was stuck pondering the questions to myself, my eyes grew heavy and I fell asleep.

Oaren and Aerian's voices met my ears before I opened my eyes and, once I did open them, I saw the two of them sitting on the large rock, crying. Jealousy hit me when I saw that Oaren shared an intimate moment with Aerian. I sat up and moved closer to them, hoping that they would pull me into their conversations.

After they ignored me for a few minutes, I decided to take the initiative. "What's wrong?"

Oaren wiped his eyes and took a breath. "We are crying for the loved ones we lost."

I looked at Aerian. I didn't know she had lost anyone.

"The Knights killed my boyfriend and the rest of the royal family, who were like family to me. I don't have anyone left." She sobbed, gasped for air, and wiped the tears away as they streamed down her cheeks. I didn't realize that this was so personal for her. I just thought that she was trying to get me to save her and the island.

"Me neither." Oaren choked back the tears threatening to flood from his eyes.

"You have me," I told them. "I'm here to help you and make things right, as much as possible anyway. But I kinda need someone to teach me the things I need to know about Atlantis."

Aerian stood up and wiped the last of the moisture from her face. "Come. We should keep moving to the base where you will meet your friends. We can talk on the way." Oaren stood up and composed himself as Aerian re-lit the torch with magic. Then we started walking again.

"I cannot believe no one gave you this information," said Aerian.

"In our defense," Oaren chimed in, "he was set on finding you and wasn't even considering becoming the Prince."

"Alright," said Aerian, "then let me explain as much as poss-ible. The leaders of this island are bred, not picked. You can only become a ruling Prince or Princess if you have royalty in your blood. The reason for that is because of a special quality in the royalty breed."

"Royalty breed?" I questioned the sound of it. "You mean they have some trait that separates them from other people?"

"Yes. You have it too. As I said, it is in the blood."

"You mean it's a gene."

She thought about the word for a minute. "Yes. A gene. It is called the *Hippocampus Syndesi.*"

"*Hippocampus Syndesi?*" I pondered that for a moment. "Syndesi means connection. I know Hippocampus as the structure in our brains that looks like a seahorse."

"Precisely, my Prince. The hippocampus in royals allows them to do three things that no one else can do. The first is that they can connect with the sorcerers and sorceresses that work for them."

"Hence our connections." It all started to make sense.

"The second is that it allows them to access the Mnemosunero and, through it, they, like sorcerers, can access memories of those that came before them."

"Mnemosunero? Memory water?" I wasn't sure what it meant.

"Yes. Mnemosunero can be created with any liquid but it needs to have a spell cast on it. You and I could access it to see any memory from anyone that we want. Oaren on the other hand, unfortunately, would only see it as a normal liquid."

I looked at Oaren, who said nothing.

"The third thing that the *Hippocampus Syndesi* does is allow the person access to the very necklace around your neck, which in turn, allows the bearer to enter Atlantis from the outside."

"And gives them visions when in water," I added.

"Aruc's Pendant is enchanted with *Mnemosunero Antigrafo*, a spell that turns any liquid to memory water. Any liquid that the jewel encounters will allow you to have visions but no one else would notice a difference in the water because they don't have the *Hippocampus Syndesi*."

"But when I was in water, the necklace lit up and formed the pictures."

"As I said, the necklace is cursed to help enhance the vision of the Mnemosunero. Since you were someone who had never connected with Mnemosunero before, the jewel did a little extra work to ensure you saw what you needed to see."

"So that helps me understand why I could connect to you with my mind and it explains the visions I had in the water. But I still don't understand why I ended up with the necklace. How did my grandfather?.." I paused but decided I didn't want to elaborate on my personal life. "...How did he end up with it and why did he give it to me? Surely there are other people that have Atlantean royal blood."

"There probably are but as I said before, there is something special about you. You are the boy predicted in the Aruc's Prophecy."

"What Prophecy? How do you know that?"

Aerian stopped. Large waterfalls covered the walls of the cav-ern and ran into large basins of water. "Tell me, Prince, do you know why the Knights of the Abyss killed the royal family? Do you know why the Knights of the Abyss were founded? Do you know why Aruc's Jewel, the necklace around your neck, was created? Do you understand why you, someone with Atlantean royal blood, was not raised in Atlantis?" I noticed she said raised and not born. Did she know the truth that I was hiding? "Do you understand why Atlantis is in this state of revolution?"

I looked at Oaren and he shrugged. "Do you know?" I asked him.

"Of course," he said, "we learn it in school."

"Do you know, Prince?" Aerian asked me again.

"Not even a little."

"Then maybe it is time you study your history."

Meleto Sas Istoria

We sat on the rocky barrier of a cavern lake, staring at the water. History was never my favorite subject but the stuff Aerian was explaining was information I needed to better lead Atlantis.

"Atlantis is over sixty-thousand years old, at least that's how far back we can trace our people. For nearly fifty thousand years, the island flourished as the most supreme government in the world. But then, just like many other civilizations, our people and rulers became greedy and unwise.

"Atlantis was plagued with a line of royals that were selfish and uncaring. Some of them, like King Atlas, wanted to conquer the world. But rather than me telling you, let me show you." She leaned over the water and sank her hand into the crystal clear liquid. Fresh and pure, it had a totally different look and smell than the water I

was used to in Miami.

Aerian closed her eyes, pushed her head back, and circled her hand in the water. "Mnemosunero antigrafo," she chanted a few times and then pulled her hand out of the water. After about a minute, ripples grew from the center of the lake and moved toward us. When the surface settled, I could see the island of Atlantis in the water.

"Incredible," I exclaimed. I looked at Oaren. "You can't see that?"

"Just water," he answered.

"I told you it is a unique trait of royals," said Aerian. She placed her hand back in the water. "And now I make sure it shows you the history you need to see."

I leaned forward and watched a movie come to life in the lake. The strange part was, I also knew the back-story, and so I narrated it to myself in my mind.

An Atlantean military general stepped out onto the balcony of the sand colored palace. His ocean blue tunic scattered with sand colored Atlantean symbols. His smooth, handsome face, blond hair, and ocean blue eyes defined Atlantean elites.

"My Lord," said the general.

"Alexios," replied King Atlas before the general could conti-nue. "How long until our military returns?"

"At least three hours before they make it to the gates of the city," answered Alexios.

"And how long until the Egyptians make it to the gates?"

"Less than that," said Alexios. "Maybe an hour and a half?"

King Atlas stared out at the island he controlled. The palace's sand colored exterior stretched around him. Palm trees growing on the grounds seemed to go on for miles. Small streams ran through the palace grounds and connected to one large river that ran under the middle of the palace.

Atlantis had borrowed the best architecture from Greece and Egypt and blended it with their own oceanic style to make a beautiful palace that shared the center of the island with the temple to Poseidon. The wall around the palace grounds was built with bricks and designed with sea turtles, seahorses, dolphins, and Atlantean myths.

The palace sat on the island's highest point, allowing for a full view of the island straight to the ocean. King Atlas saw smoke rising from the farmland and the forests of the eastern shores.

"The Egyptians must pay for this destruction," said Atlas, his

seaweed green tunic and dark hair blowing lightly in the warm breeze. His rugged face showed anger for the destruction he observed.

But if King Atlas was to be truthful with himself, he would have realized that he brought the Egyptian attack on himself. He'd allowed his greediness to overrule his logic. He sent almost the entire Atlantean military to attack Egypt and Greece and left the island of Atlantis unprotected. He wanted to rule the world and he figured Egypt and Greece were the two nations he would have to control first.

His quest for power was not a surprise to the people of Atlantis. After all, he had his nine brothers murdered so that he could become sole king of Atlantis. But the murders weren't just about power. They were also to instill fear in the people of Atlantis. King Atlas wanted the people to fear him so that they would not question his bloodlines. In fact, those that were caught questioning his bloodlines, due to the fact that he did not have the qualities of Atlantean royalty, were sentenced to death for treason. Atlas figured that if he couldn't earn their respect with his bloodlines, he would rule them with fear.

"Alexios," said Atlas, "how many casualties have we endured?"

"Thousands, my Lord," answered Alexios. "The Egyptians are sparing no one. They are killing our civilians. Men, women, and children are being murdered without the smallest amount of mercy. They are burning our farmland and forests, pillaging our towns, and contaminating our water."

"Have they made any demands?" Atlas clenched his hands tighter on the wall of the balcony.

"None, my Lord."

"Gather up all able men and prepare them for battle." King Atlas turned and walked toward the opening in the palace wall that led him inside. He stopped, just in front of the opening, and turned to face Alexios. "Atlantis does not surrender. You must hold them off until our military returns."

"Understood, my Lord." Alexios bowed and went on his way.

King Atlas took one last look at the island before heading into the palace. Fifty thousand years of prosperity were ending with the worst attack Atlantis had faced in its history. He was to blame. That thought kept creeping into his consciousness. The irony of it all, he sent his military to carry out an attack like the one he was witnessing. The difference was that if their attack took place, it would have made him the most powerful ruler in the world. This attack was weakening his power. It was destroying the most successful civilization in the world.

He had to do something. He had to put all his selfish goals aside. A fifty thousand year old civilization was about to end under his watch. And, if his military was successful in driving the Egyptians away, he would benefit greatly. He would be known as the King who saved Atlantis. And he could use the people's hatred of those countries to wage war against them. He could cover up his greed with the prospect of revenge.

But if he failed, he would be known as the King who destroy-ed Atlantis. The one who made the fatal mistake. That just couldn't be. He had to do something and he knew exactly what that was. He had to call on Aruc.

Alexios ran through the streets of the city just outside the palace walls. People boarded up their houses and businesses. Alexios understood why they were doing it but he also knew that it was useless. Boards would not keep the Egyptian army from destroying their city.

The marble buildings that stood in the center of the city might withstand the attack but not without damage. And the regular houses and businesses made of wood, rock, and clay would be destroyed in minutes. Everything he loved about Atlantis was at risk. The beautiful buildings, the long history of prosperity, the clean streets, fresh grass, and pure water were all at the mercy of the invading military. But this was his chance to prevent the destruction.

He continued running the streets, which ran out diagonal from the palace. He knew he would have to cross two rings of water and he would eventually come to a wall that separated the city of Atlantis from the rest of the island. That's where he would setup his guard. He would cut the invading military off as they attempted to infiltrate the city.

The fields could be farmed again. The forests could be replanted. But it was the city that had the most to lose. The heart of their civilization; their history and their future.

The sun beat down on his skin and mixed with the heat of his agitated body to cause him to perspire. He stopped to take a breather. After regaining his breath, he said "all able men need to report to the city wall to prepare for battle with the approaching enemy military."

Men, women, and children looked at him. Fear filled their eyes. The hope that was so well documented in the eyes of Atlanteans now gone.

He was not the top military commander and they showed him they realized that with their eyes piercing into him. It was as though they were asking him "who do you think you are?".

The top military commanders were on the ships that were hopefully approaching the island. He was left in control. It was up to him to create the civilian army that would hold off the invaders until their true military returned to the island. That idea gave him a quick boost of hope as it flickered across his mind.

"All able men from the ages of thirteen on," said Alexios, "must report to the city wall now." He was proud of himself for creating more direct instructions. He watched as men hugged their wives and children, gathered up the weapons they had, and joined in a band with their sons and neighbors to march to the wall.

A slight breeze carried a mixture of ocean and smoke as Alexios continued on his way. He knew that King Atlas was calling on Aruc for advice on how to handle the invasion. But he also knew that he had a job to do. He knew he had to setup the best defense for the city. He had a small idea that might just work.

Aruc entered the sand colored throne room. Dozens of seaweed and ocean blue colored statues decorated the room in the shapes of seahorses, sea turtles, dolphins, and fish.

King Atlas sat, tapping, impatiently on his throne. "Finally," growled Atlas.

"I was busy packing my precious materials," said the sorcerer. He fixed his gray robe and long black hair, and approached the king. His tall, thin body looked famished in relation to the bulky king. "How can I assist you, my Lord?" Aruc asked.

"What becomes of this situation with the Egyptians?" Atlas questioned. "What are they planning?"

Aruc took some sea salt out of the right pocket of his robe and threw it into the air. The salt dissolved, as if in water, and created a temporary screen in the middle of the room. The screen displayed the enemy ships sailing the five rivers toward the city. It also showed hordes of soldiers marching on foot, burning everything in their path. It was obvious to King Atlas that the invading military was close to the wall of the city.

"Their numbers are great," said Aruc. "They plan to destroy the island. And if they attack the city, they will succeed. We are outnumbered. They are determined."

"But we can hold our own," said Atlas, though it sounded more like a question. "Surely we can defend our own land?"

"My Lord," Aruc continued, "our people are losing faith. They don't see a bright future like they once did. They no longer see Atlantis as a great place to live. They are worried about being attacked. They are watching their neighbors run out of money and food. Our once strong, prosperous nation is falling fast.

"The people are watching our farmland burn and businesses collapse at the hands of the Egyptians. I'm sure all hope is lost from their minds."

"You didn't lose hope, did you?" asked Atlas. His eyes bore a hole through Aruc.

Aruc hid his hatred for the king. The king was responsible for the way people felt, but if he spoke his mind, he would be executed on the spot. "No, my Lord, I have not."

"What must I do to win?" asked Atlas.

"I have a plan," answered Aruc. "There is a chance I can save Atlantis from the enemy. But I must first return to my shelter in the dungeons to carry out a preliminary step. I will then return with further information. In the meantime, our military and civilians must drive the enemy to the coast and send them away from the island."

"That's easier said than done," scoffed Atlas.

"My Lord, it is the only way." Aruc bowed and hurried from the room before Atlas stopped him.

"I want an eighth of the men to stand just inside the gate," directed Alexios. "I want a quarter of you outside the wall to meet the incoming military. I want another eighth of you to stand on the wall, armed with bows and arrows. I want another quarter inside the rings of water on the edge of the city. An eighth will take to the rivers on ships. And the final eighth will stand just outside the palace wall."

The men stared at Alexios waiting to see if he had any further instructions. He did not. That was all he could come up with. It sounded great but it would be better if the plan involved trained soldiers and a greater number. At this point, he was looking at defending the entire city of Atlantis with just over two thousand untrained boys and men. The Egyptians were coming in a trained mass at least ten times that.

"We do not have to defeat them," said Alexios. "We just have

to hold them from the city and palace as long as we can and hope our military returns soon. Now go to your posts."

The men scattered in various directions as they followed the instructions they were just given. Alexios followed the eighth of the civilian military that headed to the top of the wall surrounding the city.

He ran ahead of the crowd and, when he got to the wall, entered the interior of the wall through a large wooden door. He took the steps to emerge on top. He had a panoramic view. The Egyptians, as he had expected, were closing in on the city. He turned around and watched as his fellow countrymen continued their preparations for the oncoming attack.

He turned back away from the city and watched the Egyptians continue their march. The civilian military, one eighth of them anyway, lined up along the outside of the wall.

"Line up in a straight line," Alexios ordered the men that were with him on top of the wall. The men did as they were directed. A few men made their way down the line, handing out bows and quivers of arrows.

The Egyptians were minutes away. Their army more visible than before. Unless the Atlantean military could return fast enough and his civilian army could hold them off long enough,

Atlantis was doomed

"Front lines," Alexios yelled as loud as possible so the men below could hear him. "Be ready!" The Egyptians ran toward the front lines. "Archers, be ready!" Alexios made the decision to engage the enemy immediately. "Front lines, CHARGE!"

Over two hundred men, from the young age of thirteen to over eighty, ran toward the Egyptians. The formation not strong enough to do much damage to the enemy but at least they might take out the first line. The sound of metal on metal met his ears; the battle had begun. It was only a matter of minutes before the Egyptians were at the edge of the wall.

"Archers," Alexios yelled. "FIRE!!!" Over two hundred arrows whizzed away from them and rained on the Egyptians. More successful than the previous attack, Alexios called for another round. "FIRE

AGAIN!!!" Another round of arrows rained on the enemy and more soldiers collapsed as the arrows pierced their bodies at the weak spot in the armor.

New Egyptian soldiers filled in for the ones that fell victim to the arrows. A few of the Egyptians made it to the gates of the wall and tried to break the wall down. Alexios aimed his arrows at the soldiers and fired; one, two, three, four arrows; each of them hitting their target. The gates were not breached.

"ARCHERS," Alexios screamed, "FIRE!!!" A third round of arrows targeted the enemy as a new line approached the gates. This time, more soldiers made it to the gate. Alexios shot as many arrows at the enemy as he could, as fast as he could, but he heard the splinter of the wood gate and the clang of the metal grate. The walls had been breached.

He turned to his civilian army standing just inside the wall. "BE READY!!!" As the Egyptians entered he yelled, "ATTACK!" His new line of nearly four hundred men met blades with the Egyptians as they entered the city.

"ARCHERS," Alexios yelled, "ANOTHER ROUND. FIRE!" This time the arrows pierced bodies on the inside of the wall, Egyptian soldiers and some of their own soldiers. There was no way to hit only the Egyptian soldiers.

The Egyptians cut through the Atlantean lines like a warm knife through butter. They weren't holding strong enough. They had to slow the enemy down and give the Atlantean military time to make it to the city. Alexios re-entered the wall and ran down the steps. He made it to the bottom and took to the city, battling with Egyptian soldiers along the way. The Egyptians that were ahead of him were killing every Atlantean they saw. This was an act of deliberate murder. This was not military against military.

He made it to the first ring of water just as the first Egyptian soldiers started to swim across. The bridge that usually allowed for easy passage was pulled up so that the enemy would not be able to cross easily. Alexios had to swim as well. But this was his homeland and he knew something the enemy did not.

He dove into the warm water and descended as far as he could go, until he met the bottom. He swam forward, along the bottom, which took him into darkness. He was under the city and the ground from above blocked all light. But he knew where he was going. He continued until he reentered water infiltrated with light. He knew that was his cue to emerge. He came up in the eastern river running through the city.

He observed his surroundings. Egyptian ships had already made it into the city and were engaged in naval warfare with the Atlantean ships manned with civilians. The Egyptian soldiers on foot were tearing through the city and minutes from the wall surrounding the sacred land with the palace and temple.

He dove back down, returned to the dark water under the city, and continued swimming until he found himself inside the sacred land. He emerged, climbed out of the water, and ran to the wall. He found a portion of his army standing just inside the wall of the sacred land. "Reinforce the gates," he ordered. He did   not want a repeat of what happened at the outskirts of the city.

"Use anything you can find to make the gates stronger."

The men started looking and Alexios entered the wall and climbed to the top. He was going to watch the enemy approach. He was going to give his men the warning they needed to be ready to engage the enemy. He could see smoke and destruction. Buildings fell in waves as the enemy approached.

Alexios looked down and found three teen boys standing at the base of the wall. "You three," he yelled to them, "come up here." A minute later, the three boys were standing next to him. All three of them were the definition of Atlantean elite. Handsome, blond, and blue eyes. The oldest was probably seventeen, the youngest fourteen.

"Go to the palace," Alexios instructed. "Find King Atlas and take him to the depths of the city. Do not stop until he is deep in the tunnels underground."

"But what if they find us?" the oldest boy asked.

"You will find shelter and reinforcements there," Alexios assur-ed them. "Now go!" The boys were gone just as fast as they had come to the top of the wall.

A few Egyptian soldiers approached the wall and Alexios fired on them to keep them from getting to the gates. He wanted to give his soldiers below as much time as possible to reinforce the gates. He knew that once the Egyptians made it through this wall, they had to cross just one ring of water before they found themselves at the palace.

As a larger line of Egyptian soldiers approached the wall, Alexios received the sign he was waiting for. In the depths of his mind, as though he was seeing it with his eyes closed, he saw the seahorse illuminated by a bright light behind it. And he knew what was going to happen next. He heard the stomps, felt the rumble of what was coming. He couldn't tell if the Egyptians realized it but they would know in just seconds what they missed all along.

The Atlantean military emerged from the inside of the wall through the gates and charged at the Egyptians before they could even reach the wall of the sacred land. Alexios smiled as he saw another wave of Atlantean military surface from the river in the center of the city. They surrounded the Egyptians that were between the center of the city and the sacred land.

Alexios also knew that the military was emerging at the wall of the city and the rivers all around the island. Because, unlike the Egyptians, he knew that the Atlanteans were in the depths of the island. Atlantis was an island floating on water but in the depths of the island lay tunnels that were created by their ancestors. Those tunnels ran from one side of the island to the other in all directions. And if you knew the map of the system, you could get to any place on the island you wanted without surfacing. And that is exactly what the Atlantean military did.

The Atlanteans drove the Egyptians away from the palace, back through the city, and eventually to the ocean. The small number of Egyptian soldiers that survived the battle quickly made their way onto their ships and sailed away. Within a few hours, Atlantis was safe. The Egyptians that had plagued the island were either dead or on a ship sailing away from the island.

"Fine job," the Atlantean commander told Alexios. "You managed to hold them off long enough for us to return." And with that, the commander walked away to help his military assess the damage and begin the repairs.

King Atlas was eating his victory dinner; delicious caviar, oysters, and squid. Thousands of Atlanteans died in the attack but now the Egyptians were gone and King Atlas had a reason to celebrate. He was going to be remembered as the King who saved Atlantis. In addition, he now had the motive to attack Egypt and conquer it. That was the very quest that he had sent his military to carry out which ended up putting them in the situation they just ended.

"My Lord," the top military general entered the room. He wore the ocean blue tunic with sand colored symbols just like the other soldiers.

"What is the urgency?" King Atlas barked. "You interrupt my victory meal and thus it better be important."

"Yes my Lord," the general replied. "The Egyptians stopped sailing. They collected their ships offshore."

"Are they threatening our shores?" Atlas questioned.

"Well, my Lord, you must come see for yourself."

Atlas pushed his food away from him and stood up. His servants scattered in chaos. Some of them cleaned up the food, others fixed his seaweed green toga as he walked.

Atlas followed the general to the balcony of the palace. He looked to the West and scanned the island, past the first ring of water and wall, and found the city folk celebrating. The general handed him a looking glass that magnified the view. He scanned over the second and third rings of water, and the wall on the outside of the city, and saw flat farmland. Egyptian ships sat off the coast, far enough to appear to be sailing away to the naked eye.

"My Lord," the general said, "not all of those ships are Egyptian. Look at the designs on the sails. Some of them are Greek."

King Atlas felt his heart collide with his stomach. The Greeks were there but they weren't engaged in battle with the fleeing Egyptians. Instead, all of the ships were sitting on the ocean.

"What would you have me do, my Lord?"

"Find Aruc," Atlas demanded. He walked quickly and powerfully back to his throne room. The general headed out of the palace to find Aruc as instructed.

"You must go," Aruc told them. "You are part of the royal bloodlines. If the Egyptians and Greeks get into the palace, they will kill you." He led a group of Atlantean royals, all with smooth, beautiful faces, blond hair, and ocean eyes, down a dark and cold hallway. He had seen this coming. He knew the Egyptians were meeting the Greeks and that Atlantis would soon be overrun.

And by that time, escape would not be an option. In fact, if they didn't hurry, the royals would be heading to their death. They weren't far from the boats but time was against them.

Seeing what was to come was Aruc's blessing and his curse. He was a sorcerer and he could see the future in his mind. He knew that Atlantis was in trouble. But he also knew that by sending some of the royals away, they would be safe and a backup if needed. An emergency plan would be in place.

They got to the pier that sat on the underground lake. "There were once hundreds of boats here," Aruc told the royals. "But many Atlanteans escaped during the attack. Now it is your turn."

He helped each of the royals; three women, three men; four boys, and two little girls; onto the boat. "Go," he told them. "Don't look back. Let the legend of Atlantis live on inside you. Don't let us be forgotten." He untied the rope from the dock and pushed the boat away. The three men and two of the boys started to row and the boat moved down the river.

"Aruc," the general said as he approached. "Here you are! I've been looking all over for you."

"Can I help you?" Aruc asked.

"King Atlas requested your immediate presence in the throne room," the general told him.

Aruc nodded and headed to the tunnel that would lead him to the basement of the palace. It only took him a few minutes to reach the throne room. He found King Atlas sitting, tapping impatiently on his throne. Aruc fixed his gray robe and long black hair, and approached the king.

"You told me you would return for the next step," Atlas reminded him.

"And so I have," Aruc replied. "The Atlantean military was successful in driving the Egyptians from the island. But now they have regrouped with the Greek military. "Everything is now in place for the next step."

"What can we do?" Atlas questioned.

"I can create a barrier around Atlantis to protect us from the outside world. I will create an illusion, make the enemy believe the island sank."

"And then?"

"And then Atlantis can continue to prosper on its own," Aruc lied. He knew that it would not prosper while under the rule of King Atlas. But he also knew that Atlas would not rule forever. "No one outside will know that Atlantis exists. They will think it is at the bottom of the ocean. We can carry on with our way of life without outside influence."

"But the decision must be made now. If I'm going to create the barrier, it has to be before the enemy attacks again."

"I order you to create the barrier."

"This is going to take all of my energy," Aruc said. "Be sure I get rest following the spell."

"You will be rewarded," Atlas told him.

Aruc walked to the balcony of the palace. He threw his hands in the air, tilted his head back, and rolled his eyes to the back of his head. With all of his concentration, he created a bubble around the island. He also made sure that the enemy soldiers saw the island sinking by creating an illusion in the bubble.

He finished creating the bubble and sinking the island in the illusion and then used the last of his energy to create a jewel. It was a silver, diamond shaped jewel, made of a metal found only on the island of

Atlantis. The diamond had a wing on each side of it. On the top part of the diamond, Aruc inserted the blue gem known as Hydrome. Then he inscribed 'Atlantis' in the metal with mental energy.

He knew that if anyone from the outside world would ever be able to help Atlantis, they would need the key to get through the barrier. And since it was created from metal and a gem found only on the island of Atlantis, it would connect the outside world to the island. He put one last finishing touch on it. He placed a spell on the jewel, "let it show royalty the world to which they belong. And so long as the royal to which it belongs lives, let it be forever attached."

"Is it finished?" Atlas asked as he approached.

"Yes, my Lord," Aruc was weak. "The barrier is in place. The enemy believes the island sank. And most importantly, the key is cut." He cast the key into the unknown and then collapsed.

The sorcerer, dressed in gray robes, pulled himself to his feet. The King had not followed through on his word. No one was around to help him. King Atlas said that he would be rewarded for putting the barrier around the island. He was rewarded, as usual, with nothing.

Aruc walked slowly, and apparently painfully, into the palace. He made his way through the throne room and to a hallway, following it until he came to some steps. There, he descended to the lower levels of the palace. He took each step with a wince of pain. The energy he put into hiding the island had weakened him. And now he was feeling the pain of an old and battered body.

The steps seemed to go on forever but when he finally came to the bottom, he followed the hallway to a room on the right. He made his way to a chair and sat down. He took a piece of parchment and a quill and began writing. I tried to force the vision to focus on what he was writing but it would not allow me to see.

Aruc finished writing, rolled the parchment up, and placed it in

a wooden box that had a painting of a seahorse on it. Then he stood and moved to the shelves on the side of the room. He waved his hand in front of the shelves and they separated from the wall. He pressed his hand against the wall and a trap door opened...

The vision ended abruptly before I could see what was behind the door. "I will take it from here," said Aerian.

"Wait," I cried, "what was in that room? What did he write on that paper? I thought you said only the royals and the sorcerers know about the underground tunnels."

"Hold on, take it easy." She stood up. "I will explain right now but we should start walking again." I climbed to my feet and Oaren did the same, though he had been sitting on a rock some distance away. "We should be able to make it to the base by daybreak if we walk without stopping."

"Fine with me," I said, "as long as you explain everything as we walk."

"I will."

We looked at Oaren. "We do not have to stop."

We started walking and Aerian started explaining. "Thousands of years ago, the military knew of these caverns. However, as the years went on and there was more fear of uprising on the island, the royals stopped informing the soldiers of the underground system. The sorcerers used magic to wipe the memory of anyone who knew about the caves that should not have known. Now the only people that know about these caverns are the royals and the sorcerers that serve them."

"But they are legend to our people," Oaren interrupted. "We discuss them as an intriguing and mysterious myth that would be incredible if real. They are real."

"The room that Aruc went into was a room deep in the palace basement that contains enchanted artifacts passed down through the sorcerers. There are items in there that could change the course of Atlantean history, even destroy it in seconds, if they got in the wrong hands. But I am certain that they are safe from the Knights. I do not expect that the Knights know the room exists and even if they do, they will not know how to access it."

"What happened to the royals that left the island? What happened to Aruc? And King Atlas?"

Aerian smiled at my curiosity. "King Atlas found out that Aruc sent royals off the island. He sent soldiers to kill the royals that left and he had Aruc beheaded for treason."

"What about the paper that Aruc wrote?" I questioned.

"I never found the parchment he wrote on. It may have been

destroyed sometime in the last eleven thousand years, or maybe someone on the island has it, but I have never been able to read it. However, it is thought that he wrote his Prophecy for the Revolution of Atlantis on that parchment."

"Prophecy for the Revolution of Atlantis?" I was confused.

"Aruc predicted that the island would have issues again. In fact, he predicted the very events taking place now." Aerian looked at Oaren. "You know the Prophecy, don't you?"

"Yes," Oaren answered.

"Recite it for our Prince," she instructed.

Oaren cleared his throat. "From blood of evil and blood of true, a boy is born and this prophecy due. For when the abyss rises to make its mark, the savior is the boy with royal blood half dark."

"I'm the boy with blood half dark?" I questioned.

Aerian shrugged. "We do not know for sure but you do have the necklace that leads us to believe that you are. Aruc cast the jewel to eventually meet with the Prince that he predicted in his prophecy. We can find out in due time when we do some family research."

So I was born on the island as a royal and I supposedly had blood that was half dark, which I didn't know what that meant. And the royal family believed that I was the Prince in the Prophecy enough to send me off the island when I was just a baby. Of course, I wasn't going to tell Aerian and Oaren that I knew about that fact. This was too much to take in. "So you're basing your decisions on the fact that I might be the Prince in the Prophecy."

"We are sure enough and we do not have much of a choice," Aerian said. "The Knights of the Abyss must be defeated."

"What about the fact that I have blood half dark?" I said. "That doesn't sound good. Why would you want to help me?"

"The prophecy states that you're the savior," Aerian said. "So regardless of what blood half dark means, the prophecy says you are the savior."

I decided to accept that answer and move on before I got too hung up on what the dark blood meant. "You said that you would tell me why the Knights formed and why they murdered the royals?"

"The Knights of the Abyss was created a few hundred years after Aruc put the barrier around Atlantis. It was formed by a group of Atlanteans that were unhappy about where the future of the island was headed. Their common goal was to expose the island to the world and try to conquer other lands.

"They increased their membership over thousands of years, though we assume they had drops in the membership as well when there were popular rulers. But the worst part about the organization is that rumor says that the founders included Egyptians and Greeks that were hiding on the island."

"I never heard that," said Oaren.

"It is thought that some Atlanteans that were unhappy with King Atlas allowed some of the Egyptian and Greek soldiers to stay on the island and they hid them from the Atlantean military. Those Egyptian and Greek soldiers had children with Atlantean women and those children were raised to have a hatred for Atlantean royalty. That hatred was passed down through the generations and eventually, it fueled the descendants of those foreign soldiers to join the Knights of the Abyss."

"They do not teach us that in history class," Oaren stated with a look of disbelief.

"History does not always tell the full story," Aerian told him.

"I know that," I added.

"There is even a derogatory name the royals use for the descendants of the Greek and Egyptian soldiers," said Aerian. "They call them murks because their lineage, like murky water, is not pure. But of course, not all murks join the Knights, in fact some of them are prominent citizens on this island."

"Why did they decide to rise against this royal family?" I asked. "Weren't they popular?"

"The royal family was very well liked," Aerian told me. "I am not sure why they decided to rise up now. My guess is that there is something behind it that we do not yet know. I do not think it is directly related to the family that was killed. I think the Knights murdered them to start their uprising because, for a reason unbeknownst to us, the time was right."

"The time was right for what?" I questioned.

"You are very curious," Oaren replied.

"I told you I wanted to know what was going on," I stated.

"The time was right for them to act," Aerian explained. "They do not believe in the way Atlantis is ruled or how it operates on a daily basis. They want to overthrow everything and run it their way and this was the time to do that. But as I said before, I do not know why this is the right time to overthrow the government."

"Unfortunately," Oaren picked up, "the Knights' way of running things is going to destroy everything that is Atlantis. They will take away our way of life and they will ruin all that defines us."

"That's why I called on you," Aerian said. "You were chosen to receive the necklace and that means that you are the one that is supposed to rule Atlantis right now, when there is no one else to lead. You're wearing the necklace; I assure you that is not a mistake or a coincidence. You have to be the Prince that Aruc predicted, the one with the blood half dark. We do not know what that means but, for now, we just have to trust that which we do not understand."

Kako Apati

I stared at the base from the outside, looking at its sand-colored stone walls. As Aerian predicted, we made it to the large hexagonal structure by morning. We had entered through its depths and walked the steps up to the main floor, where we found dozens of rooms. Once inside, the three of us tried to figure out what was taking place. As the retired soldier had promised, hundreds of men gathered at the base, collected weapons and shields, and waited for further direction.

Still, after nearly two hours at the base, there was no sign of Ries, Troy, or Broden. I really thought that they would've made it to the base before us. I sat on a bench, watching more people join our cause and thinking about how I would lead them if Ries didn't show up. He was the experienced fighter. He was the one that knew about putting together a battle plan. I didn't know any of that and I had counted on him to help me.

Aerian sat down on the bench next to me. First she focused on the activities around us but then she turned her attention to me. Our eyes met and my stomach twisted in knots. I couldn't believe my reaction, I was usually so composed around girls.

She took my hand in hers and rubbed it, which made my stomach even tighter. "They will be here." I wondered if she connected to my thoughts without me actually knowing. "We must be patient; they were in a battle with the Knights after all."

But that's exactly what had me worried. What if they were kill-ed during the fight? I didn't tell her any of that. I just sat and enjoyed the personal moment with her.

An old man approached us. I cursed him in my head for interrupting the moment but the wrinkled face with the long scar on his right cheek was familiar. Kamau, the man who took us in after the dark magicians attacked us in the city and I went unconscious. "My Prince," he said, his voice soft yet excited. "You made it! As if I had any doubt at all."

"You too. And look what you did for us; this is incredible. I never imagined you would be able to gather up so many men in such a short time."

He smiled at me. "It was nothing. I made a few contacts, they made a few contacts, and so forth. It was exponential growth."

"And who says you don't use math in the real world," I joked. No one responded. Perhaps they never questioned why they learned math or other subjects like we do in America.

"The Knights are angry," Kamau said, "and they are retaliat-ing."

I looked at him with concern. "Retaliating?"

"They see your invasion of the royal grounds and the rescue of the sorceress," he looked at Aerian, "as an uprising against their rule. They are threatening to put to death anyone associated with you."

"The soldiers I was with," I said, "are they alright?"

"I do not know," Kamau answered. "I did not see them during my journey here." He paused and waited for my emotions to settle. "But I do know that they killed the woman that owns the Moda Raftis."

I gasped with horror. "She gave me my first tunics, said they were for Prince Jedrick but they would fit me because we're built similarly."

Aerian ran off, sobbing.

"You should be careful not to reopen healing wounds," Kam-au said. "Your sorceress friend was very close to the late royal family."

"I know," I replied. "I just can't believe they killed that wo-man."

"They are sending a message," Kamau said. "They want the people of Atlantis to know that they are in charge and that supporting your uprising is a dangerous act. They are making you seem like the threat to Atlantis; like you are the rebel."

"But that's not true, they are the ones that rebelled against the government of Atlantis. They killed the royal family, not me. I'm not rebelling against the government; I'm trying to save what's left of it."

"You know that," Kamau said, "I know that, and the Knights know that but they do not want the people to know that. If they are going to rule, they either have to get full support of the civilians or they have to lead by fear. They are trying the first one now but my guess is they will eventually find that the latter works best for them."

"We're not going to let it get that far. They have to be stopp-ed."

"But we must be careful to not put anymore civilians in danger.

If the Knights can associate them with you, they will kill them to continue their message. And they will continue to make you out to be the rebel. It is what we call 'Kako Apati' and it is a technique that has been used by royals in the past."

"Well, we need to act soon then."

Kamau studied the soldiers around us. "I can get them organ-ized and settled for the evening if you like." I nodded my head. "I will manage them until you are ready to give further instructions."

"I think it's time I train for battle." I stood up. "We also need to put together a battle plan and finish recruitment."

"My friends will finish recruitment and I will help you with the battle plan. I was an adviser to the general in my prime; I worked on plans of attack and defense. We will meet in the preparation room of the base at nightfall. Until then, I will organize the soldiers and make sure recruitment continues."

"And I will find a soldier to train me."

Kamau walked toward a group of soldiers standing near the wall of the base. I slowly turned a hundred and eighty degrees and observed the events taking place. Soldiers sharpened weapons, practiced sword maneuvers, and gathered piles of other weapons, shields, and corselets. My attention turned to the large Greek columns that lined a small path to the base grounds. Ries, Troy, and Broden entered my line of vision and walked toward me.

Proponisi kai Schedio

Ries insisted that we talk in the planning room so Oaren and I found Aerian and then we met the three soldiers in the large room at the center of the base. Ries was sitting at the head of a massive wooden table; Troy and Broden were sitting next to each other, to the left of Ries.

"Mission accomplished," Ries nodded his head in approval.

"Thanks to Aerian," I told him, "she helped us find a secret passage into the palace and then she led us here..."

"He gives me too much credit," Aerian cut in, her eyes pleading with me to not say anything about the underground caverns. "Trey and Oaren were the ones that found their way to me and battled all of the Knights that were on guard."

"What happened with all of you?" Oaren questioned the soldiers.

Troy smiled. "Broden and I had a nice little fight with the Knights.

They outnumbered us ten to one but we held our own until Ries was able to divert their attention."

"The Knights have a room inside the wall where they coordinate their surveillance," Ries said. "I guess they have some pretty important information in there, but I didn't know that when I set it on fire with one of the torches they had on the wall." Laughter and smiles filled the room.

"It was brilliant," Troy expressed. "The Knights had no choice but to turn their attention to the burning room and Broden and I were able to escape. Ries got away too and we met up not far from the wall."

"We waited for you for a little while," Ries said. "After you didn't show up, we decided that you probably were already on your way here so we took the chance."

"I'm glad we have a great big homecoming," Aerian spoke up, "but we still have a major problem. We have to get the Knights out of the royal grounds so that Trey can rule from the palace."

"I know that," Ries told her sharply. He stood up, walked to a map on the right wall, and studied it for a minute. He turned back to face us. "It appears that Kamau has gathered quite a number of soldiers. He and I will work on forming a plan of attack. Broden, I want you to coordinate the men that are coming in to join our cause. I need a total number and it would be most helpful if you could split them by skill." Broden nodded and left the room.

Ries looked at Troy. "I want you to train Oaren and Trey for battle.

Give them practice with swords but also make sure they practice shielding themselves from sword attacks. It would be helpful if you teach them how to use a bow too."

"I can do that," Troy told him.

"Give them as much training as you can by sunset. At that point, we will all meet back here to discuss the plan of attack we create."

"What about me?" Acrian said.

"I want you to use Mnemosunero and Trey's map to determine how many Knights and dark magicians there are and where most of them are stationed."

I took the map out and handed it to Aerian.

"We need to split up and get to work," Ries wrapped up the discussion. "The time is going to go too fast for all that we have to do."

Troy found an isolated area at the back of the base to practice our sword techniques. The open space, surrounded by trees, had more than enough room for a sword fight. Troy motioned for us to stand facing him.

"Show me how you remove your swords from the scabbard," Troy directed.

Oaren and I acted with the same motions. We grabbed the hilt of the sword and pulled it out without much technique at all. Troy shook his head. "You are both lucky you did not cut yourselves or each other. That is not how you pull the sword out. Let me demonstrate."

He showed us the sword in his scabbard. "The sword blade must be stored facing up. When you are ready to draw your sword, you grab the scabbard in your left hand," he demonstrated as he talked, "and pull it to the side. Next, you pop the guard with your thumb, and using your right hand, twist the blade out and away from your body."

I didn't know if Oaren caught on quickly but I certainly didn't. I guess my facial expressions told Troy what I was thinking.

"Let me demonstrate again." He put the sword back and then drew it, slowly going through each step for a second time. He returned his weapon to the scabbard. "This time, practice along with me."

Oaren and I followed each step closely. "Not bad," Troy said. "Now try on your own." We both drew our swords at the same time and Troy made us do that a few times until he felt we had a handle on the concept.

"Next, you have to learn how to hold your sword." Troy drew his sword and then continued, "Wrap your thumb and forefinger below the guard first, and then the other fingers follow below them." He demonstrated what he had just said. "Next, you take your other hand and place the pommel of the sword on you palm and wrap the rest of your hand around the hilt."

I did exactly what he said and realized that my hands were curved around the body of the seahorse, not the head like when I held it before.

"Very good, my Prince," Troy said. "Your sword handling was not terrible from what I saw but I think now that you know how to properly hold the sword, you will have more control and your skills will increase greatly."

"I hope so," I replied.

Oaren had his hands clenched around the hilt of his sword, his arms straight out in front of him, locked tight. "Oaren," Troy said, "loosen your arms and hands or you will not have great control of your weapon." Oaren struggled with that but Troy took a moment to help him and he finally got it.

"Now, for making cuts, the easiest way is to think of a clock." Troy demonstrated cuts on the face of the clock, "Twelve to six, two to eight, three to nine, four to ten, and all in reverse as well." He went through it a second time. "I want you two to practice those cuts many times in the air and I want you to get faster each time. The key to life or death is not only knowing how to parry, block, slash, cut, and stab but being able to do it quick enough to catch your enemy off guard."

Oaren and I practiced the cuts for close to an hour before Troy told us to take a break. My arms ached and I needed something to drink. I returned my sword to the scabbard and then sat down on the ground, resting my back against the wall of the

base.

"I will get us some water," Oaren said and then walked away.

Troy sat down next to me. "Hopefully Oaren is better with a bow than he is with a sword." He looked at me to see my reaction; I didn't show any. "You have some natural skills with the sword but Oaren is clumsy. It will not be a good idea to put him in a sword fight with the Knights because they are very well trained."

"What do we have to practice yet?"

"I will teach you how to put your sword away and then I want to show you some defensive moves and start going through some realistic scenarios you might encounter so that you are as prepared as possible. I will battle each of you so that you can practice blocking and parrying. Tomorrow we will focus on using a bow and arrow."

Oaren returned with three cups of water and handed one to me and one to Troy. He sat down next to us. "They are really busy inside. Broden is trying to organize hundreds of soldiers into groups based on their skills. Ries and Kamau supposedly locked themselves in the planning room."

Troy stood up. "We need to continue training." He extended his hand and pulled me to my feet and then did the same for Oaren. "To return your sword to your scabbard, you bring the back of your blade on the top of your first two fingers and slowly guide the it into the scabbard." He explained it a second time while he demonstrated.

"Practice," he said as he sat down against the wall again. Oaren and I both practiced returning our swords to the scabbard without a problem.

"That was easier than the rest of the parts," Oaren said.

"I want you each to practice drawing the sword, making the eight cuts, and returning the sword," Troy instructed. "But I want you do that one at a time so you can watch and critique each other."

Oaren and I each took about a half hour to practice the whole process over and over again until Troy felt that we did the best we could, which I figured he felt still wasn't good enough.

"The most important part," Troy said as he stood up. "I will battle each of you individually and then together."

"Can we get something to eat and relax?" Oaren said. I could-n't help but agree with him. My arms throbbed and ached and my stomach growled with hunger.

"In time," Troy said, "but we need to take advantage of the time we have. You first, my Prince."

After Oaren and I both battled Troy, we called it a day. Night was fast approaching and some soldiers had prepared dinner for everyone. It wasn't anything special, they gathered up what they could, but we were all so hungry that it seemed like a five-course meal.

I filled my plate with as much salad and bread as it would hold and then looked for a place to sit. Before I found a place, Ries pulled me to the side and told me he wanted me to eat in the planning room. I headed straight for the room, where I imagined many winning battle strategies had been created, and sat down. Oaren, Aerian, Ries, Troy, Broden and Kamau all joined me within minutes, each with a plate of food.

"I wanted to have this meeting so that our Prince could get an idea of our preparation status," Ries explained. "Kamau and I created a strategy for attack that we feel will be successful. We will need a diversion."

"A diversion?" I said.

"Someone will need to distract the Knights because our goal is to get inside the royal grounds so that we can drive them out."

"I will do it," Troy said, no doubt an adrenaline junkie.

"I hoped our Prince would be part of it," Ries said.

"That is too dangerous," Aerian replied. "There is no way he should be the distraction for the Knights."

"We plan on sending Troy and Broden with him," Kamau added.

"Nevertheless," Aerian said, "he cannot be risked."

I wasn't going to make a decision without more information. "What do you expect me to do?"

"We have the Knights' outfits that you and Oaren wore to save Aerian," said Ries. "Troy and Broden will wear the outfits and they will take you to the royal grounds as though they caught you. The Knights will no doubt respond and let all three of you inside." He paused and looked at Troy, Broden and then me.

"Sounds alright so far," I told him.

"Once inside, Troy and Broden will eliminate all the Knights that pose immediate danger to you. Then they will turn their attention to opening the gate so that the rest of us can storm the grounds." Ries looked around and waited for a response.

"I do not like this," Aerian told him.

"What about me?" Oaren said. "What am I going to do?"

"Troy tells me that your skills with a sword are not up to par and therefore we hope that you are much better with a bow. If that is indeed true, we will need you with the archers." Oaren looked disappointed but said nothing.

"Aerian will be in charge of watching the map and keeping the connection with Trey," said Kamau. "She will be our link to the inside."

"How are we in terms of numbers?" I asked.

"We have nearly three hundred soldiers here at the base," Ries answered. "Broden split them into two groups; one group will be the sword fighters and the other will be the archers."

"And the Knights?" I asked.

"About half our numbers," said Aerian.

"So we have that advantage," I replied.

"But the Knights have the advantage of being in the royal grounds," Ries reminded me. "Numbers are not as important when they have the location advantage. It will be difficult for us to penetrate the royal grounds, even with the numbers we have. The city does well keeping intruders out. Which is why we planned the distraction."

Aerian's stare told me that she didn't agree with this. I didn't think it was that bad of an idea. I felt comfortable that Troy and Broden were going to protect me; the plan seemed solid to me.

"There is one problem we are not accounting for," Ries said. "As we all know, the Knights seem to be working with dark magicians."

"I can handle them," Aerian cut him off.

"They are not the problem," Ries snapped at her. "If you had let me finish, you would know that I'm concerned about sorcerers."

"I didn't think there were any other sorcerers," Oaren said.

"Surely there are," Ries said. "And I think that some of them might be with the Knights. Their magic will be much more powerful than the dark magicians, and Aerian's for that matter."

I considered telling them that I already encountered a sorceress but I didn't think telling them about Jocasta was important enough to share all of the background story that would be involved.

"I can handle the sorcerers," Aerian said.

"Well then, it sounds like we are almost ready to attack," Ries said. "Tonight we get a good night's rest and tomorrow we finish gathering supplies and training those who need it. We should plan to leave by sunset tomorrow. Of course the three of you will have to leave before the rest of us."

"I think this plan will work," Troy said. "Broden and I love causing trouble and the Prince does not seem to mind it either."

Perpato Epi O Megali Poli

The next twenty-four hours were a whirlwind. We all slept for about eight hours and then Troy trained Oaren, Aerian, and I how to use a bow. Meanwhile, Ries, Broden, and Kamau split the soldiers in the two groups into even smaller groups so that we could march on the city without being noticed.

By noon, Ries had sent a group of about fifty soldiers, both swordsman and archers, out to the city. They were to stick to the forests of the south and end up in the western farmlands. Later that afternoon, he sent two more, slightly larger groups out—one to approach the city from the northern forests and one to approach from the southern forests.

Oaren, Aerian, and I were shooting targets with the bow and arrows when Ries approached our training session. "We have a few hours before sunset and it is a few hours march to the royal grounds," he said. "I suggest that Troy gets changed into the outfit of the Knights, Broden already did, and then the three of you need to leave.

You are the start of the plan so you have to make it there before the rest of us."

Troy nodded and left to change. Ries handed me a metal corselet to put on under my tunic, for protection. He gave Oaren and Aerian one as well. "Good luck," Ries said and then he walked away. I was left standing with Oaren and Aerian.

"This is it," I said. "This is where we make everything right." It sounded corny to me but I couldn't stop myself. It just felt like the right thing to say at that moment.

"Be careful, my Prince," Aerian said and then she did some-thing I didn't expect. She hugged me. It felt so good to embrace her. I had no idea if I would make it out alive, or if she would for that matter.

"You too," I said. She released me and then walked to the base and entered it.

"Good luck," Oaren said.

"I don't need luck when I have such great soldiers surrounding me," I told him. "Keep yourself safe and remember to aim those arrows at the heart of the Knights."

"Trust me, I will. I am looking forward to making them pay for my parents' deaths."

"Me too."

Troy and Broden approached in the navy ninja suits. I stared at the silver wave on the headdresses and hoped that the Knights wouldn't recognize that these two were not really part of their group. That would surely mean instant death for all three of us.

"Are you ready, my Prince?" Troy said.

I nodded and we started our journey away from the base. We walked west, through the old marble columns and into the dense forest. We had a couple hours before we would make it to the walls and we needed to take the time to solidify our plan once inside.

"Ries told me he will be leading the last group of soldiers to the city soon," Troy told me. "He wants to attack at night fall. He told me that as soon as the last light escapes the sky, we are to begin our plan. Everyone will be in place by then."

"And what's our plan?" I asked. "I mean specifics would be nice."

"Broden and I will take your sword and we will march you to the gates on the eastern side of the royal grounds. The Knights will let us in and we will immediately kill the Knights in close vicinity. We will return your sword and it will be your job to get into the gatehouse and let our soldiers in. The gate on the eastern side is much smaller than the western side so we should have fewer confrontations."

"I hope so," I said.

We entered the city, weaving through small alleys, to find our way to the wall. We stood between two marble buildings, staring at the sand colored fortress. The sun sank slowly in the sky. My heart seemed to be counting every second I had left to live. By my calculations, I had only minutes remaining.

The sky darkened. Troy and Broden pulled their swords from their scabbards. I took mine out as well and handed it to Troy. He put it in his scabbard. "As soon as we kill the first Knights, take your sword back and head for the gatehouse."

I nodded to tell him I understood, my voice too weak to talk. They each put their sword tip to my back and, as the last light disappeared, pushed me out of the

alley and toward the wall.

The Knights on top of the wall started shouting immediately to each other once they had seen that I was held captive by two of their own. "Open the gate," one of the Knights yelled.

"Here we go," Troy whispered to me. "No turning back now." He pushed me forward, still pressing the blade into my back, as the gate rose. It was a good thing I had the corselet on or the blade tip may have punctured my skin.

We entered the grounds and the gate began to lower behind us. Three Knights approached us, coming across the bridge of the moat.

"You captured him," one applauded Troy and Broden. "Well done."

"Here," Troy said, "you can take him from here." He pushed me at the Knight and, without hesitating, stabbed his sword into the stomach of the one to his right, while Broden killed the one to the left. The one that I collided with pushed me away. Troy quickly stabbed him and then handed me my sword. He pulled off the headdress. "GO!"

I ran back toward the gate and found the door leading to the inside of the wall. The Knights on top of the wall screamed as I fought to open the door. An alarm sounded and metal hit metal behind me as the door opened, I assumed more Knights had come to battle Troy and Broden but I didn't want to look back.

Two Knights met me immediately inside the wall and I worked through the directional cuts Troy taught me, managing to fend off their slices. I blocked one sword and pushed back with all the force I could muster and then, when that Knight lost his balance, I flipped my sword in my hands and stabbed behind me. I felt the blade enter the flesh and heard the gasp of pain. I pulled the weapon out as the other Knight charged forward. I drove the blade into his chest.

I quickly spun the wooden turn wheel to my left with all my strength. A deep rumble shook the wall as the gate opened.

I headed up the nearby steps as a voice penetrated the area. "We are under attack at the eastern gate. All Knights to arms!" Two Knights ran down the steps, their swords aimed at my chest. Avoiding the weapons, I tossed them down the steps.

Knights awaited me when I climbed out onto the walkway on top of the wall. Five of them sliced at me. I fought off their weapons on their first attacks but they each came back for a second. I couldn't block five swords again so I jumped into the air and kicked my feet forward, connecting with two Knights. They both fell backwards as I hit the ground on my back. I jabbed my sword up connecting with a third Knight. The other two drove their swords at me but I swung my sword in a circle, knocked their blades from their grip, and sliced their legs. They lost their balance and fell. I scurried to my feet in enough time to stab the two soldiers I had kicked, as they came at me again.

I was free to take a moment to think. The plan called for me to leave the royal grounds once the eastern gate was open but I wanted to try to open the western gate so the rest of our military could get in. I decided to run the wall to the other side.

Voices yelled behind me and I turned to find more Knights climbing onto the wall from the same door I used to get up top. Trapped. A group also in front of me, though far enough that I had time to think of a plan.

"Trey," Ries screamed, "get out of there!" Troy and a group of our soldiers battled Knights inside the royal grounds.

The soldiers on both sides of me approached quickly. "Trey, get down!" Oaren yelled. He stood in front of a group of archers—bows drawn and ready to fire. I hit the floor as arrows whizzed up over the wall. The soldiers in front of me collapsed.

I climbed to my feet and looked over the edge of the wall at Oaren and the archers. "I'm going to open the western gate," I told them. "Cover me!" I ran the length of the wall to the western side without encountering any other Knights. Oaren and the archers had killed them before they reached me. Our soldiers on the south side joined the archers as we made our way to the gate.

Knights already outside the still closed western gate, battled a large group of soldiers. On the northern side of the wall, Knights with bows spread out to attack. I climbed into the wall and down the steps.

"Welcome, young Prince," a Knight hissed at me. Three more pulled their blades and prepared to strike.

"Give it up," I told them, "this is my palace. We're winning this battle."

The Knight laughed. "The battle has not even begun."

I charged at the Knight who laughed at me. He blocked my sword and knocked me backwards. The other three came at me and I did my best to block their attacks. My sword caught two blades at the same time but the third slashed my right arm. My flesh tore with a burn and I screamed in pain.

Ries, Troy, and Broden burst through the door and diverted the Knights' attention from me. I grabbed my arm with my left hand and held it as blood gushed from the wound and saturated every inch of skin.

More Knights tried to get into the wall.

"Open the gate," Ries said as he led the other two soldiers out into the mass of navy blue. I spun the wheel and listened for the rumbling to stop.

Trey, the dark magicians entered the battle. We are in trouble.

Aerian, where are you?

Outside the wall; on the southern side. The city is falling apart. The civilians are running for their lives. The magicians are killing everyone they find. They lit some buildings on fire. Our soldiers are trying to fight them but metal weapons are not very useful against magic and I am only one person. We are taking a massive hit on this side.

I'll be there as soon as I can.

Trey, it is no use. Try to get into the palace.

I disregarded her last statement, left the wall, and ran out through the gate.

The southern side was definitely in a lot worse shape than it had been when they covered me as I ran the wall. Buildings burned, bodies littered the ground, and I saw bright lights flash as the magicians killed soldiers with spells. It had only taken minutes for the magicians to change the course of the battle.

A wave of water rose up from inside the royal grounds and splashed down over the wall, washing some of the Knights and soldiers away. Aerian stood in the middle of our soldiers, trying to diffuse the waves as another one crashed down.

A Knight came at me and I blocked his sword. I pushed back against him and cut at him. He blocked my attack, stabbed, but I dodged the blade and swiped my weapon back at him. I sliced his side and he screamed in pain but didn't waste anytime driving his sword at my chest.

I swung my sword up, pushed his blade away, quickly got a stronger grip on my sword and drove it into his stomach. I pulled my sword out and watched the Knight drop. I decided I needed to catch my breath.

"Help," Oaren cried, surrounded by Knights. I ran to them and drove my sword into the back of one of the Knights, pulled it out and pierced another before the group that had surrounded Oaren turned their attention to me. Oaren and I worked together to take out the rest of the Knights.

"Thanks," Oaren said before he ran to help a group of soldiers that were overwhelmed. I turned to follow...

Trey!

A wave of water fell toward me. I threw my hands up as though they would protect me and waited to drown.

NIKI

The wave stopped, suspended above my hands. The water roared like a caged beast wishing to be set free. I looked to see if Aerian was responsible for saving me but she was locked in a fight with a dark magician. She threw a ball of orange light at the magician and his body disintegrated, then looked at me.

Trey? How did you?

I don't know. I just put my hands up to protect myself and the wave stopped.

Can you control it? Try moving it with you arms.

I dropped my sword and pushed my arms forward toward the wall, the wave receded. I smiled with satisfaction. This new discovery changed everything.

Let's double-team them. Work with me to control the wave and wash away the Knights and dark magicians on this side of the wall.

Alright but be careful. Magic drains you quickly, especially when you are new to it.

I turned, pushed my arms forward and pulled the wave over the wall and then swung it down to the ground. Aerian swung her arms with me and we guided the waves around our soldiers. The Knights and magicians scattered into the alleys and side streets as the water swished through like it was in a tube.

The wave dissipated into the city with the enemy. Some of our soldiers ran after them. "Let's move inside the grounds," I yelled as loud as I could to the remaining group. The soldiers ran to the western gate, yelling and screaming with their swords in front of them.

Careful, my Prince. You need to recuperate from the magic.

I'm fine. Let's go.

I picked up my sword and followed the group, Aerian right behind me.

"Archers to the top," I pointed my sword at the top of the wall once I made it inside the grounds. Oaren went up top and led the archers against the Knights that shot arrows at our soldiers.

Ries, Troy, Broden, and a small group of soldiers engaged in battle with a larger group of Knights. The soldiers that just entered with me went to their aid, and within minutes, all of those Knights were dead or had retreated out of the grounds or into the palace.

"Archers, don't allow anyone in or out," I yelled to them. Some of them continued shooting at the Knights on the wall while others turned their attention to protecting the gate.

I ran to the door in the wall and then called for Oaren's attention from on top of the wall as I put my sword in my scabbard. "I'm closing this gate and then I'm going to close the eastern one. Cover me while I run."

"You got it," he yelled back.

I went inside the wall and spun the wheel until I felt the quake of the gate hitting the ground. I ran outside and looked to the top. Oaren sword fought with a Knight. A new group of Knights somehow made it onto the wall and overpowered our archers. I feared for Oaren, knowing that his sword skills were lackluster.

Ries and his crew closed in on the palace and engaged with a group of Knights. I ran, without cover, across the grounds toward the eastern gate. Soldiers and Knights battled in front of the door I needed to enter.

Pain stabbed me square in the back and I fell, paralyzed, to the dirt. A strong air flipped me over and I found myself face to face with a woman. Her black, tied up, hair matched the color of her outfit. Her outfit like the ones the Knights wore, only she didn't have a headdress. No doubt, this was the woman that I met at the pool. Jocasta.

My muscles wouldn't work as her silver eyes pierced into me. Acid burned my skin, or at least that's how it felt. I screamed out in excruciating agony.

The woman laughed the most evil laugh I'd ever heard; a hundred times worse than the most evil laugh in movies. Cold vines ran down my back but I couldn't even shiver. "We meet again, young Prince," she hissed at me in Atlantean and laughed again. "This time you have nowhere to go. You and your friends greatly underestimated the power of the Knights. They have resources you cannot even imagine."

I wanted to yell back at her but found my vocal chords useless.

"Hundreds of years of recruiting, planning, and patiently collecting weapons and resources, have led the Knights here today. You have only scratched the surface of this organization. A new swarm of wasps over took this hive and all you did was irritate them.

"Speaking of wasps," she kicked dirt up into the air, "let me know how it feels to be stung by a swarm. *Sminos sfika.*" The particles she kicked into the air became black wasps and flew toward me. My mind pushed and twisted at my muscles but yet I lay motionless. The swarm sped towards me like darts toward a corkboard. I could only imagine what I would have sounded like if I could make any noise at all.

Water rose out of the moat, Aerian guided it into the air and then pushed it toward me. "*POULI*". The water turned into a dozen birds and they dove at the swarm of wasps. The swallows ate all of the stinging insects before they could reach me and then they liquidized and crashed to the ground as puddles.

The furious woman turned to Aerian and shot a ball of purple light at her. Aerian caught it and threw it back. Aerian tossed yellow light at me and I felt my muscles loosen. The ball of purple light flew back at Aerian with even greater force than the first time. Aerian caught it but it blew up in her face and she collapsed.

I climbed to my feet and tried to stabilize my wobbling legs. Jocasta turned to face me. I grabbed air while focused on the fire of a burning torch on the wall. The fire streamed to my hands and I collected it into a large ball and then tossed it at the woman.

She threw her hands up and water flew from the moat and extinguished the fire, leaving a cloud of steam in the air. "Magic?" she hissed. "You *are* a special boy."

Ries led a group of soldiers yelling toward us. The woman vaporized into the air, mixed with the cloud of steam, and crashed into the moat. Gone.

I ran to Aerian who seizured on the ground. "Aerian, can you hear me? What can I do to help?"

"What do you want us to do?" Ries asked me. "There are no more Knights out here. They are all either in the palace or they fled the grounds."

I focused on Aerian but I knew he needed an answer. "I need to tend to her," I told him. "Storm the palace and get rid of all the Knights inside. Take all of our swordsmen but leave the archers on the wall."

Ries nodded and then ran toward the palace. I could hear that he was yelling to the soldiers but he was too far away for me to make out the words.

"Aerian," I pleaded, "please speak to me."

"Close the gate," she whispered. "Finish this battle."

I wanted to stay and help her but she was right. The gate need-ed to be closed before the Knights and dark magicians that escaped came back.

"I'll be right back." I ran into the gatehouse and spun the wheel until the gate hit the ground. Then I went back to Aerian.

"Is it over?" she said in a weak voice.

"The gate is closed. Ries and the swordsmen are checking the palace for Knights."

"Good. It is time that you have your own palace bedroom for a good night sleep." She smiled and I laughed.

"What did she hit you with?"

"It was a very powerful weakening spell."

I swallowed hard, my throat burned. "Isn't there something we can do?"

"I will be alright," she said as she grasped my hand. Hers was ice cold. "I just need to let it wear off with rest."

I breathed a sigh of relief; I had expected the worst.

"Go," she said, "check out your new palace. Make sure the battle is over. You need to rest and then the real work begins."

I smiled at her to hide my nervousness. I now had to restructure a government, win the confidence of an entire population, and make sure that the island of Atlantis moved forward. And I had no idea how to do any of that.

"Come on," I said as I lifted her up, "you're coming with me." I carried her to the steps of the palace.

"What are you waiting for?" Aerian asked.

I had butterflies in my stomach. I was about to step inside the palace. My palace. A large, sand colored building with thousands of years of history. Inside, I would be ruling Prince. It would be for real. The Knights were gone and it was now my government.

"I'm just taking it all in," I told her and then climbed the steps and entered the palace.

Inside, the soldiers rejoiced. "Niki!" They smiled and clapped for me.

The main hall was expansive and marbled with large columns on either side.

"Ries is in the defense room," a soldier told me, pointing to the room directly ahead. I carried Aerian into the diamond-shaped room through a door to the left of the point. I set Aerian down on a chair.

"Niki!" Troy ran and hugged me.

"The Knights are out of the palace," Ries told me. "We check-ed every room on this floor and upstairs. Soldiers are now in the basements looking for any remaining enemies. Most of them probably escaped by river."

The room stretched into a hallway at the other diamond point.

I walked into the hall and found a glass wall opposite the defense room. I stared at a beautiful courtyard. The moonlight reflected on a pond in the center.

I returned to the room and sat down at the large wooden table, similar to the one at the base in the southeastern forest. I yawned; the exhaustion had suddenly caught up to me.

"You need to get some rest, my Prince," Ries said. "Our sold-iers will stand guard at the wall and I will make sure some stay in the basements as well. We are safe now."

I nodded, pleased to finally be done with the battle.

"Tomorrow will be a busy day for you," Aerian said. "The people will expect a speech. But for now, I will show you to your room." She stood up slowly and led me out of the defense room, to stairs, and up to the second floor.

My body must have shut down as I followed her to the designated room for the ruling Prince. I barely even focused on removing my belt, sandals, and corselet. My mind shut down right as I hit the bed.

Epanasynedo

Sunlight filtered into my eyes as I woke up. I sat up and observed the room around me. The king size bed with dark blue sheets and drapery sat just off the center of the room. Above the bed, a glass window allowed sunlight to flow in. Large cabinets and dressers made of the same wood as the table in the defense room rested along the walls.

The room had to be the size of all the rooms in the center of the first floor. The sand colored walls had splashes of ocean blues and greens and featured various paintings of sea life. The soft ocean blue carpet cushioned my feet as I stepped onto it.

I pulled the tunic tighter around my waist and then walked toward the eastern side of the room. A glass circle in the floor, just past the base of the bed, made me stop. I stood on the glass and looked down at the courtyard, the same courtyard I had stared at last night from the hallway inside the defense room. "This is incredible," I said to myself. "I need to check that courtyard out."

The open sliding door in the eastern wall allowed a breeze to flow through a screen. I opened the screen and stepped onto a large balcony overlooking the eastern side of the city and island. In the distance, over the buildings and miles away, I could see the Atlantic Ocean. "Oh, I could get used to this!"

I looked over the side of the balcony and saw two giant seahorse statues supporting it. "I could spend all day out here." But first, I wanted to explore the rest of the palace so I headed back inside and slipped on my sandals.

I found steps and a hallway outside the door on the northern side of the room. I followed the hall, passing three rooms that I assumed were for the rest of the royal family. At the end of the third room, the hallway opened up into a large area and then to a balcony. A bridge stretched across to the balcony and, standing on the bridge, I looked down on the first floor and saw the thrones.

The balcony gave a view of the western side of the island over the royal grounds and wall, through the city, across the farmlands, past the forests to the Atlantic Ocean. The beauty of it all made it hard for me to want to go home.

I walked across the bridge. Aerian stood on the other side.

"You slept long," she said.

"I don't know what happened. I just crashed."

"The magic wore you out but the adrenaline of the battle last-ed until it was all over and you were in the palace."

"I don't understand my magical ability at all," I told her.

"You are quite the mystery, Trey Atlas. I am sure we will learn more soon."

Her comment made me uncomfortable but instead of showing that, I changed the subject. "Speaking of learning more, do you know anything about the woman that paralyzed me?" I figured that if I played dumb, I might get the answers I wanted. Those answers included how much Aerian knew about my life.

"All I know is that she is a very powerful sorceress. She was able to turn nonliving dirt into living wasps with little effort. Turning abiotic to biotic is the hardest magic there is. When I charmed the water into swallows it took all of my energy, which is why I couldn't counter her weakening spell for long. But she continued to use magic. Very powerful indeed; I hope we do not encounter her again."

Considering I had encountered her twice, I knew we didn't see the last of her but, again, I kept that to myself. "She told me that we underestimated the power of the Knights. She said that they have recruited, collected resources, and planned for hundreds of years and that we only scratched the surface. That's when she said that they were a new swarm of wasps that took control of this hive and all we did was irritate them. Then she sent the swarm of wasps at me."

"Well we sent the Knights fleeing for their lives. And she left didn't she?"

"Only after she realized that I also could control magic and the soldiers joined me. She said that I was a 'special boy' and then she mixed with the steam in the air and crashed into the water."

Aerian gasped. "She turned herself into non-living particles? That is even more advanced magic. She is definitely someone we have to be concerned about."

"Let's head downstairs and find the others. I want to start talking about what we need to do to get this government up and running."

"And give a speech to the people."

"Yes." I led her to the steps along the left wall and we took them downstairs. The kitchen was to our left and statuary hall pointed out in front of us.

"Let me show you the throne room quickly," Aerian changed our direction. We walked into the throne room, the large room on the western side of the palace. I looked up and saw the ceiling of the upstairs floor and the bridge stretching across to the balcony. On this floor, sat two large thrones made of gold with ocean blue fabric for comfort. A door in the western wall led outside to a garden of flowers and shrubs.

"The royal gardens," Aerian said when she saw what I was looking at. "The most beautiful gardens on the island."

I walked over to the thrones and stared in amazement at the detail. "They don't look very comfortable." I said.

"They are for show," Aerian said. "Go ahead, have a seat. The one on our left is yours now. The other will be for your Princess, when you marry."

My princess? When I marry? It was strange enough to have a throne for myself.

"Sit," she reiterated. I did and found the throne much more comfortable than it appeared.

Aerian bowed to me as Ries, Oaren, and Troy entered the throne room and they bowed as well. "You don't have to bow to me," I told them.

"It is protocol to bow to the ruling royals when they are on the throne," Ries said as he stood up.

"A delicious breakfast has been prepared for us," Oaren said. "Please join us in the dining room."

The dining room had a large marble table with marble chairs, but luckily the chairs had padded seats and backs. A grand chandelier made of gold and diamond hung above the table. The food on the table included eggs, freshly baked bread, sausage and a crisp fruit salad.

"I want to hear your thoughts on the military," Ries started the conversation after everyone had filled their plates and started eating.

"I want archers on the wall at all times," I told him. "I want guards at both gates and on the steps of the palace, as well as just inside the palace doors. Figure out a rotating schedule for our soldiers. I want you to get a list of every registered soldier."

"Any boy over the age of seventeen is registered," Ries said.

"Then I want to see records of every boy over seventeen. Is it policy that they have to serve in the military?"

"It is current policy, yes," Ries answered.

"Then I want you to make sure they are all trained and separated based on skill. But I want only the best soldiers to protect the royal grounds."

Ries nodded in agreement. "You really should talk to your top general."

"I am," I told him. "You *are* the top general overseeing the entire Atlantean military. That is, if you want the job?"

"I would be honored," Ries said with a smile.

"Troy and Broden will be next in command. They will each have two jobs, as far as I'm concerned at least. Troy will be in charge of training and the guards. Broden will manage recruitment and he will be responsible for placing soldiers in the appropriate job within the military."

The three soldiers were amazed that I gave them the honor. "As soon as the three of you are comfortable in your new positions, I want you to hand pick the people to work under you so that your jobs are not overwhelming."

"What about Kamau?" Oaren said.

"Kamau headed home," Ries told us. "He is retired and would

prefer to not be part of the military anymore."

"Aerian, I want you in charge of everything to do with magic and sorcery. I want you to lead a team of soldiers, which Ries will handpick, to find and arrest anyone who practices dark magic or sorcery." She nodded. "I also want you to keep an eye on my map to make sure our enemies do not resurface."

I looked at Oaren. "You will have the most demanding job and also the most important one," I told him. "You will be responsible for the every day activities of this island when I am not here. You will manage everything as though you are the Prince when I am at home. While I am here, you will be the person I talk to about everything. You will be my second in command."

"When you are not here?" Aerian exclaimed.

"I am not of royal blood," Oaren reminded me.

"You're blood doesn't matter to me but your loyalty and sacrifice does. Please accept the position."

"I will," he told me.

I looked at Aerian. "Believe it or not, I actually have a home I have to go to from time to time. I have friends and family that I can't abandon forever. Besides, I have to get back to school. I plan to go home tonight."

"What?" everyone in the room called out at once.

"While I am gone, you can get started on your jobs. Oaren, I need you to find staff for the palace. We need cooks, gardeners, servants, and others to maintain this palace while we run the island."

"You cannot leave before setting up a structured government," Aerian pleaded.

"The government is structured. You all know what to do. Follow the policies already set in place until I evaluate them. I have faith that Ries, Troy, Broden, and our soldiers can maintain the peace and keep everyone safe while I am gone. The people of Atlantis will not even know that I'm gone."

"You must speak to the people," Aerian said. "They deserve to hear from their new Prince, to put their fears to rest."

"I will speak to them this afternoon," I told her. "But then I'm going home. And I imagine you can help me get home."

She nodded.

"Oaren, after you finish breakfast, I need you to make the announcement that I will speak at dusk." He agreed and I stood up. "We all have plenty of things to do. I'm heading to my room to work on a speech."

I stood over the glass circle in the floor of my bedroom looking at the courtyard and trying to finalize my speech to the people of Atlantis. I wanted them to know that I was here to help them and I was going to do everything in my power to protect them and prevent another uprising from the Knights. While everything I thought sounded good to me, I didn't understand why the Atlanteans would even want to listen to me.

The light above faded as the sun inched to the horizon. It wouldn't be long before I had to make my speech. A knock on the southern door interrupted my thoughts. "Come in."

Aerian entered, wearing a new, pink dress, with a seaweed green tunic in her arms. "Time to get dressed," she handed me the clothes.

I walked behind the dressing curtain and stripped out of my old tunic and replaced it with the new one.

"I do not know if I can handle being in this palace," Aerian said, with sadness in her voice. "My family is gone Trey and now you are leaving too."

"Only for a little while," I told her as I pulled the tunic as tight as I could around my waist and then pulled the top over my head. "I have some things to take care of at home but I'll come back."

Aerian sat on my bed crying when I walked out from behind the dressing curtain. I sat down next to her. "Hey," I said with concern, "it's alright. I promise I won't abandon you." She sobbed even harder. "Besides, I look forward to the cries in the water."

She looked up and cracked a small smile through the sobs.

"You have to heal," I told her. "I understand that. Take as much time as you need. But remember, I'm here for you. All you have to do is call."

The smile grew a little bigger and she stood up. "Time to make the speech."

I stood up next to her and she fixed the top part of my tunic, still too short for my tastes. Then she fixed my hair and observed me carefully.

"How do I look?" I asked as I spun around for her.

"Like a prince."

"A good looking one?" I smiled.

"Trey, all of the royals were beautiful. But there is one thing you are missing."

"What's that?"

"The royal tattoo."

The balcony on the western side of the palace hosted chairs and Troy, Ries, Broden, and Oaren already sat in them. Two archers stood on each side of the balcony and numerous soldiers stood guard down below, as well as a dozen or more archers on the wall of the royal grounds. Hundreds, maybe even thousands, of people waited outside the wall. The noise could be compared to the crowd of a professional football game.

"How can they hear me?" I asked Aerian.

"Leave that to me," she said.

Oaren stepped to the railing of the balcony and Aerian went to him and touched his neck. She came back and did the same to me. A sensation tickled my throat and I tried to clear it, the sound echoed in the distance.

"Your voice is magnified," she told me.

"May I have your attention?" Oaren said in Atlantean, his voice filling the island. "It is with great honor and pleasure I present the new Ruling Prince, Trey Atlas."

"Remember to translate to Atlantean before you speak," Aerian told me.

I walked to the railing and stood next to Oaren. The crowd chanted "niki" and my gut twisted. My body shook harder than ever before.

I took a deep breath and translated my thoughts. "Thank you!" I put my hands up and signaled for them to quiet down. The noise decreased slowly. "Last night we witnessed a great victory indeed. However, this victory is not mine. This victory is yours!"

"Niki" chants started again.

"You have all made incredible sacrifices. You remained calm during a very turbulent period. The royal family was ruthlessly murdered and you were subjected to the horrors brought on by the Knights of the Abyss. But you pulled out strong. As I said, this is your victory.

"Before I continue, I would like to have a moment of silence to pay respects to the royal family, civilians, soldiers, and royal servants that lost their lives during the unfathomable attack." The crowd went silent and, after a minute or so, I continued.

"It is time to move forward. We will never forget what happ-ened but we must ensure that the future of Atlantis is bright and prosperous. You are a resilient race of people and I am privileged to lead you. It will take time, but I promise that we will get back to normal.

"I'm already working with top soldiers to ensure the protection of the island and all of its inhabitants. We will not allow another uprising by the Knights. I will provide a more detailed plan in time, once all of it is worked out. For now, I will say to all of you that you are safe and that we will work together to make things right again. Thank you!"

I waved to them and then backed away from the railing while the "niki" chants resumed. Aerian touched my throat and the tickling sensation returned.

"You are not done yet," she told me. "It is time for you to be branded."

"Branded?" I said in fear.

She pushed me to the railing again. "With the tattoo I was talking about."

"Now our Prince will receive the mark of royalty," Oaren shouted to the crowd. "He will be branded with the hippocampus forever more."

A man I never saw before came onto the balcony and toward me. He must have seen the fear in my eyes. "This does not hurt, my Prince. It is a special pen that marks your skin permanently." He held my left arm still and drew an impressive seahorse that stretched from my elbow joint to my shoulder.

The man bowed before he walked away. Oaren turned back to the crowd. "Let everyone recognize Trey Atlas as our new Ruling Prince as he is blessed with the royal blood and marked with the

honorable hippocampus." Oaren led everyone in a bow to me.

The last rays of light faded fast and the people returned to their homes. "Not that it matters much," Oaren said after Aerian removed the voice spell, "but you are now the official Ruling Prince."

I smiled. I was proud of what we had accomplished and relieved that we took control of the palace. "I hate to rush it," I said, "but I think it's time I go home." There were many things I wanted to accomplish in Atlantis, namely finding my real parents, but first I wanted to settle everything at home and then I could come back to Atlantis indefinitely. That way I would have the time to search for my parents.

"We need to go to the courtyard then," Aerian said.

The moonlight illuminated the quiet, cool courtyard. The perfect place to say goodbye.

"I know you never said a word to me," I looked at Broden, "but I appreciate all of your help over the last few days and all of the work you will do while I'm gone."

"Ora kali," Broden said and then left the courtyard.

"My brother barely ever talks," Troy said as he stepped up to me. "But I know that he is honored to serve you, as am I. In fact, I am happy to carry out the jobs assigned but I was wondering if I might have an even more important job."

"What's that?"

"Protecting you, my Prince. It is the job Ries assigned me when we first found you in the forest and it is a job I take very seriously."

I remembered Troy standing on the bank of the river as I washed off. It felt like forever ago, even though it had only been a few days.

"I wish to be your sole protector," Troy said.

I smiled. "I am honored and grateful to have you protecting my life.

The job is yours but please carry out the other duties while I am away." Troy bowed and, when he stood up, I hugged him. I realized then that you form a special bond with the person responsible for keeping you alive.

"Ries," I said, "thank you so much for leading us to victory."

"You are not bad yourself, my Prince," Ries said. "At least for an untrained royal."

"I trained him," Troy took offense.

"And you did a great job," I told him.

"It was an honor and I am happy to continue leading your military," Ries bowed. "I await your return." I hugged him and he patted my back three times and then stepped away.

Oaren came over and hugged me. "It was not easy but we did it."

"You were forced to sacrifice greatly," I said, "and you came out strong and proud. I am glad that you chose to continue helping me. Your parents would be proud."

As soon as Oaren stepped away, Aerian embraced me with tears streaming.

"Your sacrifice was great," I told her. "You lost your entire family and yet you still pulled yourself together enough to call on me. You have a selfless and strong soul."

"You walked away from your family, friends, and home to save a complete stranger," Aerian said, "that statement goes for you too."

"I didn't want this job in the beginning but I'm glad I followed through because it allowed me to get to know all of you. Each one of you means a great deal to me and I will come back."

"You should go," Aerian put her hand on my chest, felt for

Aruc's jewel, and pulled it out from behind the fabric. "I will put a spell on it that will allow you to return home from the lake here in the courtyard."

"Thank you."

She rubbed the jewel and murmured, "epistofi stin patrida." She looked into my eyes. "All you have to do is chant the spell once you are in the lake and picture a body of water near your home. Your hippocampus will do the rest to connect you. When you are ready to come back here, hopefully sooner than later, submerge in water and chant the same thing, only picture this lake."

I nodded but said nothing and then lowered myself in the water. I dove down, closed my eyes, and reassured myself that it was time to go home. I pictured the school's pool that I swam in everyday, kept the image in my mind, and then said "epistofi stin patrida"

Back Home

I was deep in water; I swam up, surfaced, and searched my surroundings. I was in a pool; the school's pool. The lights were out and no one was around. The world outside the windows was dark, just like it was in Atlantis when I left.

I swam to the side of the pool and lifted myself out. I was happy to be home and surrounded by the familiarity of the pool I spent practically every day in. And at least I wasn't under attack like I was a few days ago in this very room. Even though I felt like I needed to be home, there was a piece of me that already missed Atlantis and my new friends there. At least I knew that they were safe. And I also reminded myself that I was back here to finalize things before making a permanent move to Atlantis. After all, Atlantis was my birthplace.

With that, I had a sudden urge to see my family, even if they were my adopted family. Plus, I wanted to get changed back to my normal clothes. I quickly left the school and ran the mile and a half to my house. The lights were out and the door locked. I rang the doorbell and waited but no one answered the door. I knew Maria probably went home by now but I was surprised my parents weren't home.

I made my way to the back of the house and took the key from the container under the deck. I went back to the front and opened the door. "Hello?" I called. No light, no sound, no movement other than my own. I closed the door, turned on the living room light, and then went straight to my room.

It felt so good to shower in hot water and scrub myself clean with soap and shampoo. I rested in the warmth and waited, expectantly, for Aerian's cry. But unlike before, she didn't call me; she had no reason to call. My necklace was lit but didn't provide an image of any kind. The island was in peace and everything was normal again.

After about twenty minutes of letting my body relax and re-fresh, I stepped out and brushed my teeth. Then I happily dressed in my best pair of jeans and a shirt. My body felt renewed as I went downstairs but I felt like something was missing. I figured it was that I didn't have a chance to tell anyone about my adventure. Unfortunately, they still weren't home.

I didn't want to wait any longer to talk about Atlantis so I walked to Coal's house. His mom answered the door. "Trey," she exclaimed and signaled me to come in. I entered the house and she closed the door. "How are you? We were so worried about you after what happened during the swim meet and then you disappeared."

"Um, I just needed some time to recuperate," I answered, trying not to stumble in the lie. "I'm better now."

"I'm glad to hear that. Coal and Ashley will be so excited to see you. They're downstairs."

I made it halfway down the steps before Ashley tackled me and squeezed me with all of her might. I lay on the steps, it was rather uncomfortable but, I loved having Ashley in my arms. She looked incredible and smelled great.

"I missed you *so* much," she said, squeezing even harder.

"I missed you too," I replied and rubbed her back. I wanted the moment to last forever but it was already over.

Ashley pulled away and then grabbed my face. She turned my head every which way and inspected me closely. "Good, you didn't mess your face up."

Coal helped Ashley get to her feet and then extended his hand to pull me up. "How are you?"

"Better."

"So," Ashley cut in, "your parents told us you were sick but we know that's not true. Where were you?"

"I was in Atlantis."

They both looked at me in awe. "Atlantis?" Ashley questioned. "As in the myth?"

"A lot happened since I talked to you," I said. "My parents told me I was adopted."

"What?" Coal exclaimed.

"I'm from Atlantis."

"As in..." Ashley tried to cut in.

"As in the myth, yes," I told her. "Apparently when I was born, my family sent me off the island so I would be safe. Grandpa Atlas is actually the sorcerer that brought me here to find a place for me to grow up. But now Atlantis needs my help. Turns out there's a Prophecy that predicts my birth and help in saving the island."

"So you found this out and then you went to Atlantis?" Coal asked.

"Well I stormed out on my parents when they told me all of that and I went to the school's pool to swim and think. While I was there, I was attacked by one of the Knights of the Abyss, which is the group trying to destroy Atlantis. A sorceress came through a portal after him and they tried to take me to Atlantis but Grandpa Atlas, who's not really my grandfather, stopped them and sent me through another portal. I ended up in Atlantis."

They both still stared at me, their jaws agape. "We better sit down," I told them, "this could be a long story." We sat on the couch and I explained everything, starting with meeting Oaren and his family, the Knights killing Oaren's parents, the rescue of Aerian, and the final battle that drove the Knights out of the royal grounds.

"So you're the ruler of Atlantis?" Ashley questioned, as though the numerous times I stated it didn't register.

"Yeah. I'm the leader of Atlantis."

"That's awesome!" Coal said.

"So what are you doing here?" Ashley asked, with hurt and anger in her voice. "Shouldn't you be ruling your island?"

"I left Oaren, Aerian, and Ries in charge for now. They'll call me if they need something. I needed to see you guys and let Mom and Dad...let them know I'm alright. Besides, I can't miss that much more school."

"Call you?" Ashley said. "Like a royal cell phone?"

I laughed. "No. Atlantean royals have a connection with sorcerers called the *hippocampus syndesi*. Aerian will be able to call me through our mind waves. Besides," I said as I pulled Aruc's jewel out from under my t-shirt, "I can see Atlantis anytime I want. All I have to do is put this in water. It has the *mnemosunero antigrafo* curse on it."

"The what?" Ashley and Coal asked at the same time.

"*Mnemosunero antigrafo*," I reiterated. "The memory water copy charm. Any water that comes in contact with this jewel becomes memory water, which allows me to see what happened in Atlantis. I can even see memories as they are made for instant insight into what is happening on the island."

"You're so weird," Ashley said.

"I think so too," I responded.

The door to the basement opened. "Ashley," Coal's mom called down the steps, "your parents are here to pick you up."

"Listen, before you go," I said, "you two have to swear to keep all of this a secret. I don't want the world to know about Atlantis. Give me your word."

"You have my word," Ashley said.

"Mine too," Coal added. "Besides, who would believe me if I told them? They'd think I was crazy or something."

"See you guys." Ashley grabbed her purse, hugged Coal and then me, and left.

Coal sat down on the couch and I took the chair across from him. "Now that she's gone," he said, "tell me about the girls in Atlantis.'

I chuckled. "They're hot."

"Come on," he said, "you're the Prince so you have to have more than that."

"Well, there is the sorceress, Aerian. But she just lost her boyfriend and family in the uprising so I don't think she's looking for love."

"No one else?"

"No." I paused and waited for him to question but he said nothing. "So how many times has Jessica asked you about me?"

"Only a million," he answered.

"That's all," I laughed, "I would've guessed so much higher."

I sat with Coal another hour talking about old times before we said goodnight and agreed to meet at school in the morning. I didn't want to tell him that I planned to move to Atlantis permanently. It wasn't the right time to talk about wanting to find my real parents. I figured that he wouldn't understand since he wouldn't know what it felt like to be adopted. Time would let my old relationships change and my new ones build stronger.

As I approached my house, I saw that the lights were now on. I hurried to the door and entered. Mom and Dad jumped out of their seats in the living room. Mom ran to me and wrapped her arms around me; she squeezed me even tighter than Ashley.

"Thank God you're safe," Mom cried. "We had no idea what happened to you."

"Sit down," Dad said, "we want to hear all about it."

Mom released me enough so that we could walk to the couch but she wouldn't let go of my hand as I told them all about Atlantis, pretty much the same thing I told Ashley and Coal.

"So it's true," Mom exclaimed when I just finished, "Atlantis exists."

"And you say that you're the...ruling Prince?" Dad didn't understand.

"I'm a king, except they don't call them kings anymore because of the bad history they had with their rulers."

"So you make the decisions that govern an entire island?" Dad questioned.

"Pretty much, yeah."

"Do they realize you're only sixteen?" I could tell Dad didn't like the idea of me being a ruler.

"Yes. I have plenty of people to ask for help. I have Aerian, Ries, Oaren, Troy, Broden, and others. Besides, I have royal blood."

"You led them in a battle against the...Knights of the Abyss...and ran them out of the royal grounds?" Dad still wasn't sure.

"Yeah. We won the battle and the Knights fled."

"So who's ruling now that you're here?" Mom asked. I could tell she understood it and accepted it a lot easier than Dad.

"Aerian, Oaren, and Ries. Aerian will connect with my mind like she did before I left if they need something."

"This is incredible," Mom said.

"Yeah it is," I replied.

"And you're alright?" Mom questioned. "I mean, considering everything you learned before you left."

"I'm learning to deal with it," I told her. "It's going to take time to get used to the fact that my real home is in Atlantis."

"You know that you'll always be our son," Mom told me.

"I know," I said. "I love you guys and I'm grateful for all you did for me while I lived here. But I think my true place is in Atlantis. That's where my heart is now. I have a lot to do there."

"I don't want you to leave," Mom said, "and I know Dad doesn't either but we also know that we can't stop you from being part of the world you were born in. It wouldn't be fair to you or the people of Atlants and we love you too much to do that."

"Well I'd like to get things finalized around here and then I want to go back to Atlantis. I plan to make that my permanent home but I'll come back to visit everyone here. And you can come visit me."

Mom nodded. "It's going to be hard to not have you here but that's what's best for you. And I'd love to visit Atlantis."

"I want to talk to Grandpa...the Sorcerer. I want him to hear what happened and see if he wants to go back to Atlantis with me.

"Maybe you should tell Coal and Ashley first," Dad said.

"They already know," I told him. "I went to Coal's when I came home and found out you weren't here."

"Well at least wait 'til morning," Dad replied.

"He will want to know as soon as possible." I stood up but Mom didn't release my hand.

"Trey, sit down," Mom said with sadness in her voice.

"What is it?" I asked without sitting down. "Is he alright?"

"Please sit down," Mom reiterated.

"I'm going over there." I tried to pull my hand away from her.

"Trey, Grandpa's not home," Mom told me.

"What? Where is he?"

"He's in the hospital," Dad jumped in. "He got very sick after you left and they put him in the hospital."

"What's wrong with him? Is he going to be alright?"

"They don't know what's wrong with him, Honey," Mom said. "They are running all kinds of tests. We didn't want to tell you when you first returned; we wanted to wait for you to get settled."

I sat down next to Mom and cried. Now I regretted leaving for Atlantis. I could've been here when he got sick. Biological or not, he was my grandfather. This news just strengthened that fact. Blood didn't mean anything. "Will he be alright?"

"Trey," Dad said, "Grandpa lived a long, full life."

"Will he be alright?" I yelled through the sobs.

"Well he took a turn for the better this afternoon," Mom said, "but they don't think he's going to make it."

I pulled my arm away from Mom and ran to my room. I crashed onto my waterbed and sobbed. I now understood how Aerian and Oaren felt; I now connected with them on a different level. I wanted to go back to Atlantis to see them, give them support, and receive it from them. But before I headed back to Atlantis, or even back to school, I had to see Grandpa Atlas. First thing in the morning I was going to visit him and tell him all about Atlantis. He'd be excited to hear that I'm the ruling Prince and happy to find out that his sacrifice of leaving Atlantis all those years ago finally paid off.

But that didn't really matter now; my life was changed forever. No more would I be the kid with the perfect life. It didn't matter anymore if I had straight 'A's, was a champion swimmer, or had model looks. All of that was incidental because I was adopted, Grandpa Atlas was dying, I belonged in Atlantis, and my job there was only beginning. Something told me the fight to save the island that was in my blood was far from over. The Atlantis Revolution had only just begun.

A Magical Lantern That
Could Reveal Atlantis

A Family He Knows Nothing
About

A Secret That Could Steal
His Throne

THE SECOND BOOK OF THE ATLANTIS REVOLUTION

ECHINODEA

The Atlantis Revolution Continues

About the Author

At 28 years old, Tom Tancin is an accomplished author. Having already written seven books (and self-published three), Tom ventured out to write a young adult fantasy series in the summer of 2009. A fan of Atlantis, Tom decided to focus the series on the mythical island and then designed Trey Atlas, the sixteen year old protagonist of the series. Tom then spent nearly three years developing, plotting, writing, editing, and promoting the first book, *Hippocampus*, before it was released on April 3, 2012. The series is currently planned to have four books, one released each year from 2012-2015.

Tom lives in Pennsylvania with his green-cheek conure, Harley, and cat, Govie.

Visit www.tomtancin.com to keep up with Tom's progress and his latest publishing schedule.

Hippocampus **Summary**

An Island that Shouldn't Exist...

A Life He Didn't Know...

A Destiny That Can't Be Escaped

There was no turning back. We were going to set into motion a revolution that could either save Atlantis or leave it destroyed in the process.

Sixteen-year-old Trey Atlas' known life is a lie. While he was raised in Miami, Trey was actually born in Atlantis. Sent off the legendary island as a baby for his own safety, Trey is the only living heir to the Atlantean throne. Whether he likes it or not, Trey has to go back to his birthplace and accept his role as the Ruling Prince and lead the revolution to defeat the Knights of the Abyss. Otherwise, thousands of innocent lives and his true family legacy could be lost forever.

www.theatlantisrevolution.com

Made in the USA
Charleston, SC
04 October 2014